TOTLANDIA

THE ONESIES - BOOK 3 (SPRING)

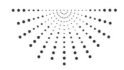

JOSIE BROWN

SIGNAL
PRESS

Library of Congress Cataloging-in-Publication Data is available upon request

Cover Design by Andrew Brown, ClickTwiceDesign.com

Trade Paperback ISBN: 978-1-942052-37-1

V102817

cheering for them and feeling all the emotions alongside them. I loved the variety of characters, the balance of funny and serious moments, and just the wacky story. I cannot wait to see what is next in the series!

—The Book CellarX

"When you think 'mom' you probably envision a sweet, cookie-making, nurturing type, but hang out on a playground for half an hour and you'll realize moms can also be catty, competitive and incredibly judgmental. Josie Brown has that bunch nailed in her new book series *Totlandia*. Picture Desperate Housewives and *Sex and the City*. *Totlandia* would be the babies they'd create. The book is a blast, packed with humorous punches between these ladies whose very existence relies on their ability to keep up appearances. This author will have you howling as you devour this most recent work. Yeah, she's that good. And so are her books.

—*Stress Free, Baby*

"Who knew that joining a mom and tot group would be so strife with maneuvers worthy of a presidential campaign? Membership in The Pacific Heights Moms & Tots Club supposedly can guarantee a bright future for your offspring. Although these women are mostly wealthy, there are a few that are just getting by. As the group opens up to new members, each mother has only one goal: to insure their

child will have every advantage that money can and can't buy. I adored this quick read and can't wait to get further into the lives of these women. There are some really sweet moments mixed in with the catty wonderfulness that Brown always seems to capture. I just can't believe I have to wait until the installment which will be released soon."

—*Mary Jacobs, Bookhounds Reviews*

NOVELS IN THE TOTLANDIA SERIES

The Onesies - Book 1 (Fall)

The Onesies - Book 2 (Winter)

The Onesies - Book 3 (Spring)

The Onesies - Book 4 (Summer)

The Twosies - Book 5 (Fall)

The Twosies – Book 6 (Winter)

The Twosies - Book 7 (Spring)

CHAPTER ONE

Wednesday, 2 January
4:55 p.m.

In clear defiance of the Bettina Connaught-Cross's edict, Bettina's sister-in-law, Lorna Connaught, rounded up her friends in the Pacific Heights Moms & Tots Club Onesies group to inform them that Kelly Bryant Overton had been dismissed, and therefore, their memberships in the club, and hers, were now guaranteed.

The relief on the faces of Jade Pierce, Ally Thornton, and Jillian Fredrick was all the proof she needed to know she'd done the right thing.

Her aching concern over a far bigger issue, her one-year-old son's well-being, numbed her own joy. Dante had recently been diagnosed as autistic.

She'd held back this knowledge from her husband,

Matthew, only to have him overhear her discussion on the matter with Dante's doctor.

Stunned by the news, it had left him helpless.

Since then, she'd punished his inability to accept this new reality with her silence.

But now, it was time to go home and face the music. To come clean with him and to express her own sorrow and shame over her duplicity about Dante's condition.

The expansive Tudor home Matthew had inherited from his paternal grandmother sat on the highest crest of Vallejo Street—east of Van Ness, on the block between Jones and Taylor, right where Vallejo plummets into Ina Coolbrith Park before emerging out the other side, in the neighborhood of North Beach.

Had the Summit—the residential high-rise, which was home to a few of San Francisco's swells, including Matthew's sister, Bettina, and her family, four-year-old daughter, Lily, and her husband, Art—not blocked them on the north side, their home's panoramic vistas would have been a complete three-hundred-and-sixty degrees. Instead, they made do with a slim peek-a-boo view of San Francisco bay, albeit one that afforded them a straight-on shot of Alcatraz, Berkeley and Mount Diablo beyond.

Matthew, sitting by the living room's large picture window, stared out at a cargo ship that was inching its way through the sailboats dotting the bay. When Lorna entered, he didn't move. She stood there motionless, resolved not to say anything until he turned around on his own. Their mutual silence transformed the room into an echo chamber for Dante's insistent humming, making it sound much louder than it really was. They'd always assumed his drone was the start of infant babble they'd heard from other children his age. How they longed to hear those sounds from Dante. Now they knew better. Maybe someday he'd talk, but no time soon.

Finally, Matt turned his swivel chair in order to look at her.

Lorna stared at his face. "You've been crying," she said. It wasn't a question but a declaration.

"Okay, yeah. I'm upset! What did you expect? I just found out—from a doctor I'd never met, at a damn *New Year's Eve party*, no less!—that my wife's been hiding the fact our son is autistic!"

"Matthew, please! I've only known for a couple of weeks. And I was going to tell you the next day, in fact! I just... I just didn't want to ruin the holiday."

He shook his head in disbelief. "To hell with 'the holiday!' What about the rest of our lives?"

"Believe me, Matt. It's a blow to me, too. But we both have to be strong, if not for our own sakes, then for Dante's."

Instinctively, both of them looked over at their little boy. By now they'd become used to his unfathomable gaze. Now, knowing that his face might never express laughter or tenderness, or for that matter, pain, their hearts ached that much more.

"Lorna, answer me truthfully. Why is it that you've never introduced me to your family?"

"I... I guess I figured you'd find them too unorthodox.

And heaven knows Eleanor and Bettina would find something to hate about them."

"Hey, you don't have to tell me. All my life I've been on the receiving end of their disapproval."

"They both adore you, Matt. You know that."

"Is that what you think? Admit it, Lorna. I've never lived up to their expectations. Then again, I've never lived up to yours, either."

She knew she should say something, that he wanted her to protest, to prove him wrong.

Instead, she said nothing. If she denied it, she'd be lying. They both knew that.

Finally, he shrugged. "And yet knowing all my faults, you married me anyway."

She shook her head in disbelief. "Is that what you think? That my goal was to marry a rich slacker, have a child with him, then pawn any genetic issues he may have, God forbid, as yours?"

"In your opinion, I'm just 'a rich slacker?'" His smile was thin and cold. "I'm glad you've finally come out and said it."

"Okay, yes, I admit it. I don't think you're living up to your potential. Heaven knows you've got all the brains and money and connections to do so." She wiped away a tear. "Still, that's no reason to blame me for Dante's autism."

"Lorna, try to hear me out. All I'm trying to say is that I"—he paused, as if considering the best way to put it—"*I thought you had leveled with me, too.* I thought since you were —you know, 'perfect,' it could make up for all my bullshit. I could hold my head up high, because you'd be there for me, to set things straight. Hell, even Eleanor has come to realize you're damn close to perfect. At least, as close as anyone who would've married me can be. I guess we were both wrong. No one is perfect." He looked down at his feet. "I know you never talk about your family because there's some pain there. It's why I've never pushed you on the topic. But now, I need you to be honest with me. Is there anything I need to know about them?"

She shook her head angrily. "What exactly is that supposed to mean? Are you insinuating that I've been hiding some deep, dark family secret?"

"Don't twist this around on me. All I'm trying to do is to make sense out of this. All I'm asking is if—well, if you have a family history of this kind of thing. I looked it up, and there is some genetic correlation."

"Whoa! Wait a minute! I'm guessing there are as many broken branches on your family tree as there are on mine." She poked him in the chest. "Look, Matt, if you want to spread the blame, start by holding up a mirror. How about all that pot you smoked in high school and college? And what about all the times you refused to hold Dante when he was an infant? Don't you think that could have a negative effect on his development?"

"That's my point! *I never said I was perfect*. But at least I've been honest about it."

"I am *so* out of here!" She started for the front door.

"*What?* Wait! You don't get it!"

But yes, she understood perfectly. He wanted her to fess up. About her parents. About her past.

She couldn't do it. Not now. Not when anything she said or did could stain Dante, too.

She looked down at her son. No matter what his issues were, he was still the one love of her life. He was still her whole world.

At that moment, she knew what she had to do.

But she couldn't do it with Dante in tow. She turned back to Matt and thrust Dante into his arms. "Take care of him until I get back."

Before his shock thawed into concern for her and the doubt she knew he felt for himself showed, she ran out the door.

CHAPTER TWO

Thursday, 3 January
10:13 a.m.

THERE COMES A TIME WHEN EVERY WOMAN MUST FACE ONE simple fact: *she is not happy with the life she has created for herself.*

For Bettina Connaught-Cross, this realization came to her during the first of her three dry cleaning errands.

In San Francisco's Pacific Heights, dry cleanliness was next to Godliness. The fourteen laundering establishments, located just down the hill within Cow Hollow's thirteen-by-four-square blocks, made the adjoining neighborhood a Mecca for those who, like Bettina, obsessed over the meekest shadow of a stain, be it on a couture frock or her reputation.

Bettina's first stop was the Peninou French Laundry and Cleaners, where her silk blouses were waiting for her. She was just about to hand the cashier her claim ticket when the little voice in her head first whispered, "It's okay for you to cry."

Bettina's hand froze.

The woman waited patiently for a moment or two. Then, very gently, she pried the ticket from Bettina's freshly manicured fingers.

Bettina pretended to be miffed and accused the woman of smearing her nail polish, but in truth, she was embarrassed to have someone witness her despair. She grabbed her blouses (on hangers and secured in couture breathable bags) and stormed out the door.

She had almost reached the threshold of Deluxe Cleaners just one block over, where three of Art's suits were waiting for pickup when the voice added, "And with all you do for him, how could he have done *that* to you? And with *her* of all people!"

Bettina knew the *he* and *her* the voice inside her referred to. Just seventy-two hours ago, as the clock was striking midnight on New Year's Eve, she had walked in on Art screwing her supposedly oldest and dearest friend, Kelly Bryant Overton.

During the Connaughts' annual New Year's Eve party, of all times and places.

And that wasn't the worst of it. While in the throes of some grotesque act of sexual debauchery, Art declared his hate—not anger or even disappointment, but *out-and-out loathing*—for his wife.

Bettina fled before either of them realized she was in the room.

To top it off, Bettina knew she wasn't the only one who had walked in on her husband *in flagrante delicto*. Lorna Connaught, her sister-in-law, whom she despised, had run out of the adjoining bathroom just prior to Bettina walking in.

The next day, Bettina had said nothing to Art. Ironically, he'd been blissfully unaware of her silence.

Was he also completely oblivious to her pain? Perhaps her recent Botox injection, which helped to keep her brow placidly wrinkle-free, made it impossible for him to notice her shock and awe at his betrayal. And no doubt he presumed her stoic demeanor was proof of her post-party contentment.

It was all she could do to keep from punching him square in the gut so that he'd truly feel her pain.

The past two days had passed in a fog. But this morning, as the founder and leader of the Pacific Heights Moms & Tots Club, she had to smile through her anguish while she led the club's "Top Moms Application Committee" in a vote to eliminate one of the five probationary members in the club's most junior families, those in the Onesies.

Both Lorna and Kelly were in this group.

Needless to say, Kelly had been duly ousted.

The official reason (Bettina would have been horrified to tell the committee members anything approaching the truth) was that Kelly had cheated by getting professional help with her probationary challenge—hosting the club's after-Thanksgiving potluck.

At their ladies' lunch yesterday, Bettina had enjoyed informing Kelly she knew about her and Art, and that she was now exiled from the club. Bettina's goal was to crush Kelly like a bug under her Louboutin bootie, dissolving Kelly to tears.

Instead, the traitor had the audacity to smile triumphantly at her…

And to hand Bettina *a paddle,* inferring that she used it on Art.

Art liked to be beaten? How disgusting!

How tempting.

As Bettina stepped into The *Ooh Là Là* French Cleaners to pick up her Irish lace lingerie and Lily's ballet skirts, she was almost afraid of what else the voice would say to her. Would it chastise her for being oblivious to the crumbling state of her marriage? Would it hint at other disasters to come?

Would it remind her that, had their roles been reversed, Bettina would have blackmailed Lorna?

But no, this time the little voice's counsel was inspiring. "Don't forget. *You are Bettina Connaught-Cross.* Your people made their fortunes during the San Francisco Gold Rush. You got rid of Kelly. Without the club, she's nothing. You're married to a partner in one of the city's most prestigious financial firms. Now you have something you can hold over him. You've founded a club in which other women fight to join. And you can also keep Lorna from betraying you by pretending to give her the only thing she ever wanted from you… acceptance."

By the time the *Ooh Là Là*'s clerk handed Bettina the hangers holding her lingerie, she felt invincible again.

She was just about to walk out the door when she noticed she was missing something. "Excuse me, but my claim ticket included my daughter's ballet skirts."

The clerk's blank stare earned her a snarl from Bettina. "I don't have all day. Go back and find them. Chop chop!"

The woman scurried away. Within five minutes, the line for pick-ups was out the door. The grumbling from the store's other patrons might have earned them an apology from anyone else, but not Bettina. Lily's tiny chiffon wraparound skirts were priceless, not just because they had been specially fitted and imported from Paris, but because of the joy it gave her precious child.

Finally, the clerk reappeared, box in hand. Bettina practically ripped it from her. She lifted off the lid, perused its contents, and slammed it shut again. "What are you trying to pull? These aren't my daughter's!"

"But… you said ballet skirts!" To prove her point, the woman lifted the lid and pulled out a tiny pink skirt.

Bettina glared at the woman. "Yes, but my four-year-old would never wear *pink*! She is serious about her art. Her skirts are black."

"I'm sorry, but we don't seem to have them."

"If you don't, it's because you've carelessly handed them over to someone else. Or maybe you've sold them. I presume, then, you know how much they're worth."

The clerk shrugged. She'd had enough of Bettina's guff. Considering she also had a wrestler's girth while Bettina sported a minus-two frame in designer couture, no doubt if push came to shove, she could take Bettina three out of three moves.

Instead, she pointed to the sign over the doorway, which read:

THIS ESTABLISHMENT IS NOT RESPONSIBLE FOR ANY LOST, STOLEN, OR DAMAGED ITEMS.

Bettina crooked a finger at the woman. The clerk hesitated, but the rumbling from the restless crowd left her no choice but to lean closer. The room went dead silent as Bettina declared, "If I find out you've given my daughter's skirts to some other little girl, I *will* hunt you down. No matter where you go tonight after you leave this dreary little job—to the Mission, perhaps? The Outer Richmond or the Tendernob? No matter. I will follow you to your slum hovel. And when the time comes for you to pick up your measly belongings and make the inevitable move in your little hobo existence, I will find you. Look over your shoulder because I will be there, too, making your life miserable. *I. Will. Haunt. You.*"

The woman didn't shudder in fear or even blink.

Instead, she smiled.

Then she tapped her nose with her middle finger.

The crowd behind Bettina roared with laughter and applause.

Despite this, Bettina walked out with her head held high.

She waited until she was a block away before collapsing onto the doorstep of a Victorian walkup.

I've lost it, Bettina thought as she sobbed. *I've lost everything! If I can't scare a dry cleaning clerk, how will I be able to keep the PHM&T members in line?*

Worse yet, how would she break the news to Lily that she'd lost the little girl's most prized possessions?

Despite the pep talk from her internal voice, the discovery of Art's affair had devastated her. Most assuredly, the upheaval in her life was *his* fault. To top it off, he wasn't even an attorney. If he had been, she could have at least threatened to sue the cleaners for every dime it was worth.

The sorrow and the pity of her predicament left her hollow. Or maybe it was the fact she hadn't eaten all morning. She craved something. Appreciation, perhaps. Love, most definitely. No, something else…

Cake.

She remembered passing a bakery just a block up on Union Street.

While she baked Martha Stewart-worthy delicacies for her family, all of her life she had eschewed sweets, knowing full well that allowing even one tempting morsel to cross her lips would wreak havoc on her mannequin-thin frame.

To hell with that. She was always sacrificing for others. Marrying Art had been a sacrifice. Having a child had almost sacrificed her figure, but she discovered a Method Nazi to whip her quickly back into shape within a month. And she couldn't count the number of sacrifices she'd made for PHM&T.

So why should she care if no one else did?

Bettina practically ran to the bakery.

&

"A CUPCAKE, PLEASE. THE CHOCOLATE ONE, THERE." BETTINA jabbed her finger at the top shelf of glass bakery case.

The jacked twenty-something manboy behind the bakery counter did a double-take. "You mean the carob 'pupcake' right? And like I said, it's carob, not chocolate. Cocoa can kill your dog. Your breeder should have told you that."

Bettina frowned. "*Dog?* No, the cupcake is for me, and I'd like a chocolate one."

The clerk laughed appreciatively. "Yeah, I know! The stuff in here looks good enough to eat, doesn't it? Take a peek at this one." He pulled a cake box off the shelf behind him and held it open for her. The round cake's caramel-hued icing had been whipped into stiff waves and was inscribed

Happy Birthday, Wags!

For the first time since New Year's Eve, Bettina laughed out loud.

She turned back around to read the signpost protruding from the shop's bay window:

Le Marcel Bakery for Dogs

She took a good look around the shop. Her mistake was an easy one to make. Small tables bore trays of what looked like bonbons and cookies. One open box was labeled "ruffles" and held what could have easily passed for chocolate truffles. Tins of delicacies that looked like biscotti and bags of tiny pretzels filled the shelves along its sweet pink- and coco-hued striped walls.

Granted, the number of patrons with fluffy little dogs tucked lovingly in the crux of their arms should have been a giveaway, but this was San Francisco, where pet-friendly merchants were the rule, not the exception. And in most cases, four-legged friends were treated better than some people.

Deservedly so was Bettina's opinion.

The clerk's grin was tantalizingly flirtatious. "Still want that pupcake?"

No, she thought. *Instead, I want someone to play with, someone to cuddle.*

Someone worthy of my love and devotion. I want someone who will love me unconditionally. And forever.

"Maybe," she answered him in the coy, breathy voice she hadn't used in ages.

Not since she'd set her sights on Art.

I sure know how to choose 'em, don't I? she thought, as the vision of Art rose in her head.

Yes, it was Art alright. *Making lust to Kelly.*

Right then and there, she decided she wouldn't make the same mistake twice.

At that moment, a man walked into the shop. The dog with him was a grand beast, long-snouted, tall, with a massive chest and a thick, bushy coat, the color of rust. Had it not been walking on all fours, it could have passed for a bear.

Bettina glanced at the clerk. As tempting as he was, males with four legs were much more loyal than those with two.

And easier to discipline—and neuter.

As for getting a female dog, no way. Bettina knew there was room for only one bitch in the Cross household.

Bettina honored the clerk with a come-hither smile. "I'll need a puppy first, won't I? So, tell me. Where do you think I'd find one like that big boy over there?"

The clerk nodded appreciatively. "Caligula? Yeah, he's a beaut, alright! A Tibetan mastiff. In fact, I know his breeder. And you're in luck. Mama's got a litter due any day now."

Bettina watched as he scribbled a name on one of the bakery's order forms. His fingers were large and thick.

Nothing like Art's.

But as tempting as the manboy was, Bettina knew a puppy was a much better way to go.

Less *merde* to clean up after.

Besides, she couldn't wait to tell Lily they were getting a dog. It wouldn't make up for the lost ballet skirts, but hey, it was time Lily learned that life was filled with tradeoffs.

The newest members of the Pacific Heights Moms & Tots Club were about to learn that as well. In hindsight, the Onesie members' initiation had been a cakewalk. Why else would Lorna have made it through and with flying colors?

Well, no more pussyfooting around. It was time to make

the Onesies members prove they were truly worthy of the honor of belonging to PHM&T!

And Art would learn his lesson, too, most certainly the hard way.

The paddle in Bettina's purse was just one of the ways she could prove her point.

CHAPTER THREE

Friday, 4 January
8:14 a.m.

"What do you mean I don't qualify for unemployment benefits?" Jillian Frederick's hand was shaking so hard she could barely hold the phone to her ear.

It had taken her almost an hour to get more than an automated voice on the line, someone who could actually answer her questions about how to file a claim. Within that hour, her cell phone beeped because its battery was low. To top it off, someone had just texted her. No doubt the waiting text was zapping her juice as well.

"Sorry, my dear, but them's the breaks." The Unemployment Office clerk practically yawned in Jillian's ear. "You worked for, like what... two months? And for minimum wage at that. What did you expect?"

"My husband left me and our two babies a few months ago. It was the only job I could find!"

"Seriously, hon, I feel for you. But I'm not Dear Abby, and the Unemployment Office isn't your parents' ATM."

"This is an emergency! I may lose my house! I supported my husband through college, so I'm sure my benefits from back then still count, don't they? Listen, can you check and see how far back you can go?"

Just then one-year-old Amelia yanked a branch of the Christmas tree so hard that three glass ornaments fell and cracked. Both she and her twin sister, Addison, wailed in union.

As Jillian scooped both girls up into her arms to cuddle them before they grabbed at the glass shards, the cell phone fell out of her hand, hitting the cold marble floor with a loud *crack*.

"Oh my God! Are you—are you okay?" Jillian could barely hear her own voice over her daughters' wails.

"I think you broke my eardrum," the clerk finally retorted.

"I'm so sorry! One of my daughters almost pulled down our Christmas tree." Jillian was trying with all her might to keep the tears out of her voice. "Listen, isn't there any way to find out if those benefits are still good?"

"Yeah sure. What's your maiden name?"

"McKeever."

"I'll check. Let me put you on hold again."

"*Hold?* Oh my God, no! My phone battery is dying, and I

was on hold for forty minutes before I reached you! Can't you just call me back? *Wait!*"

But it was too late. She was being serenaded by a symphonic version of the Black-Eyed Peas' "Boom Boom Pow."

Frustrated, Jillian fell back onto the couch. The drop in altitude left the toddlers giggling. They smacked Jillian's face as if that would relieve her too-early-in-the-morning exhaustion. She sighed, forced her lips into a smile and wiped the tears from her eyes before opening them.

Truth be told, even if she hadn't been canned, Jillian's credit card bills were mounting so fast that no amount of generous tips could've saved her. She was now four months behind on her SUV's payments. She hid the car in the alley behind her house so she could dodge the repo man who kept knocking on the door. As it was, she barely used the damn thing, except for Costco and Wal-Mart runs.

Last week she had just managed to scrape together the money to pay the gas and electric bill. To keep them under fifty dollars a month, she closed off the vents in every room of her rambling mansion on Pacific Street except for the kitchen and the nursery, where for the most part Addison and Amelia slept and played, or burned used paperbacks in the old home's fireplaces.

She had traded the convenience of her pricey local Whole Foods and the neighborhood grocery markets on Union, Polk, and Chestnut streets for Chinatown's vegetable markets, where produce could be purchased for less than half the price.

The thought of collecting unemployment benefits shamed her. But it was going on three weeks since she lost her job, and she had to do something, anything.

She was too proud to give up the home she had so lovingly restored. Further, it would have been one more intolerable defeat at the hands of her two-timing husband.

A commotion coming from the alley behind her house roused her from where she sat prostrate on the couch. She picked up both girls before walking to the window, just in time to see her SUV being hoisted onto a flatbed truck.

She set the girls down in their playpen and ran down the stairs and out the side door. The tow operator, a large bear of a man sporting tattoos on every inch of skin not covered by his jeans or the jacket emblazoned with *Bay Area Repo*, had already chained down her vehicle.

Jillian grabbed his arm. "Wait! That's my car! Where do you think you're taking it?"

The man shrugged. "Back to the dealership. Sorry, lady, three missed payments means they own it again."

"How will I get around without it? It's the only transportation I've got, and I have two toddlers! Please—"

He looked down at her. "Nothing I can do about it. Here's a tip, though. Next time, disengage the GPS so we can't find it so easily. Just sayin'."

If only she'd known that earlier.

She watched as he backed the truck through the alleyway before gunning it down Pacific Street. Then it occurred to her that she'd left the kids alone inside. Both were now adept at catapulting themselves over the playpen's side with a kamikaze flip they'd learned from their little gal pal, Zoe Thornton. She ran back into the house.

Too late. The girls were toddling toward the Christmas tree.

She grabbed them just before they hit the field of broken glass.

Now, for her cell phone. Where had she put it?

It took her a full five minutes before she realized she'd tossed it into the playpen with the girls. By the time she did, it was too late. The damn battery had gone dead.

She threw it back down into the playpen.

Big mistake. The girls climbed down out of her arms and into the playpen after it. She was just about to fish out all three one more time when the doorbell rang.

Who the hell could it be now? Jillian wondered. Before she opened the door, she looked through the peephole.

Scott.

She slumped up against the wall. What the hell was he doing there? Well, at least his pregnant new fiancée, Victoria, wasn't with him.

Not that she'd dare show her face round Jillian. The last time she did, Jillian slapped it, hard.

Then she ran before the police got there.

"Jillian, I've been trying your cell phone all morning. I know you're in there. I saw you go in after the repo guy pulled out."

Just great, she thought. Knowing he'd witnessed her losing the SUV made it all the more humiliating. She swallowed hard. "What do you want?"

"I...I left something in the closet of my office. The Apple MacBook Air, the one that looks like yours? I'd like to get it, if you don't mind."

"No, you're not coming in here. Besides, if you left anything here, I probably threw it out already." Really, she hadn't touched the damn thing. In fact, she hadn't been near the room he'd made his home office. It reminded her too much of him.

She was glad the girls were in the kitchen. If they heard their father's voice, they'd be calling his name. She couldn't bear the thought. She didn't want to let him in, let alone back into their lives. Not after he betrayed and deserted her.

Not now that he was preparing for the son he'd always wanted.

"Go away," Jillian shouted.

"For once, try to be reasonable. I need it!"

Fuck that, she thought. *And fuck you.*

"Jillian, please don't make this any harder than it has to be." He sighed. Then, as if he were trying to reason with a child, he added, "Also, I've got something for the girls."

She looked through the peephole again. True, there were gift bags in his hands.

Words danced on the tip of her tongue. *What they want most is something they'll never have again: their father...*

But what good would that do?

Besides, it had been a lousy Christmas. The girls were too young to know it, but that didn't make it easier for Jillian.

Unless she could find another job quickly, without Scott's support, all their future Christmases would be just as glum.

Scott had proven to be a lousy husband. But he was also the only financial lifeline she had in her life. As much she wanted to forget him, a tiny part of her still held out hope that he'd come to his senses and come back to her. That he'd realize the mistake he made in leaving them and ask her forgiveness. That he'd beg her to take him back.

Maybe... just maybe...

She opened the door slightly.

He held out the bags. "For the girls. Just a few things I saw in a store window and picked up for them."

She grabbed the boxes out of his hand. Through the tissue paper, she could see a tiny pink and yellow plaid coat. In fact, there were two of them: double-breasted with pink and yellow bull's eye buttons, and Peter Pan collars.

They were adorable.

She looked at the bag. The coats were from Dottie Doolittle, a children's boutique in the Presidio Heights neighborhood of San Francisco.

"Scott, tell the truth. Did you pick these out yourself?"

His hesitation told her all she needed to know. Victoria had chosen the coats for the girls.

For *her* girls.

She imagined Victoria's disgust at having been coerced by Scott to buy the gifts. Jillian knew Victoria hated her and the girls.

No way in hell would they ever wear these coats.

She threw them in his face, slammed the door, and locked it tight.

"Okay....you're right. Victoria picked them out. But it's the thought that counts, isn't it?"

"You've already gotten them a gift. It was a DNA test, remember?"

He was silent on the other side of the door.

"By the way, when are you and your pathetic brother, Jeff, going to have your tests?" Jillian taunted him. "Are you stalling because you know the results will show he's lying? Ha! I can't wait to see you eat crow for trying to get out of providing child support to our babies."

"There is nothing I'd rather do more. In fact, my test is tomorrow. But unfortunately, Jeff took a teaching job in Japan. He's not expected back until the middle of May."

Jillian snorted. "Ha! A likely story."

"I'm serious! As much as it disgusts me to think of you and Jeff screwing behind my back, I'd hate it even more if the girls... if the girls weren't mine." Even through the thick oak door, she could tell he was all choked up. "Look, Jillian, I never wanted it to come to this."

"You should have thought about that before you got your assistant pregnant. Oh, and by the way, once again for the record, Jeff and I never had sex!" Jillian hit the door with her fist, hard. She tried to rub away the pain.

If only it were just as easy to rub away her heartache.

"Jillian, please... Can I have my old laptop now? It's important! Please?"

She thought for a moment. Then, with a shaky voice, she muttered, "Wait out there. I'll go and get it."

She stumbled upstairs to his office.

The computer Scott was looking for had been purchased along with a twin, for Jillian. They were a couple of years old now. It had been a joint celebratory gift, when Scott made partner at the financial firm where he worked.

In the past, all the family photo .jpegs from their digital camera had been uploaded into her computer, which also held her favorite recipes, her email correspondence, and anything pertaining to their family life.

He should have photos of the children, she thought. *I doubt it will change his mind about me, but some day he may regret having left the girls. I'd rather he still cared about them, even if he no longer loves me.*

Jillian opened her computer. In a moment she downloaded the file containing the family photos onto a thumb drive.

She took a wild guess at the password to Scott's computer: *JackNicklaus*

Everything about him was just too obvious.

When she put the thumb drive into his computer, she noticed he'd already set up a file labeled *Photos.* So, he's already downloaded their family pictures? She wondered.

She opened the file and opened the first .jpeg.

It was a nude photo of Victoria.

She opened another. And another.

Raunch, raunch and more raunch.

In one, Victoria had a vajazzle. Its jewels spelled out *Hole in 1!*

Really? Barf. Truly. *Barf.*

Jillian tried hard not to throw up in her mouth.

He hasn't used the computer in two years, thought Jillian. *And yet all that time he had been screwing Victoria!*

She was ready to fling the computer against the wall when she had a better idea.

Scott's brother, Jeff, was the family's techno-geek. In fact, while surfing on their couch those few months in which he claimed to have had the affair with Jillian, he tried hard to convince both of them to open secured accounts with a digital cloud company, where the files could be uploaded for safekeeping. To get Jeff off her case about it, she reluctantly agreed. Now cloud computing was second nature to her.

Obviously, Scott had never moved his files onto a cloud, or else he wouldn't be bugging her about the computer. That was par for the course. Scott was always of the mindset to let others do the grunt work for him.

The way he'd convinced Victoria to buy the girls' Christmas gifts was a great example.

Well, Jillian had a gift for Scott, too.

In a flash, all the files on his computer were uploaded into her iCloud account. It took just few moments to erase everything off his computer's hard drive: his financial reports, work assignments, and certainly those files with the nude shots of Victoria.

The only thing she left him was the Excel spreadsheet containing his old golf scores.

She ran downstairs, opened the door and thrust the computer into his arms.

"Get the DNA test, so we can all get on with the rest of our lives," she commanded.

She didn't wait for him to respond, but slammed the door as hard as she could.

Then she dropped to the floor, crying.

Amelia and Addison's tiny hands, patting away her tears, brought her back to reality. At noon, the Pacific Heights Moms & Tots Club was holding a special initiation luncheon for Onesies candidates who had successfully completed the challenges assigned to them over the holidays. She had to pull herself together and get the girls ready.

Smiling through her tears, she announced to her babies, "Let's play dress-up!"

She watched, brokenhearted, as they squealed and nodded. Then she took one plump little hand of each girl, swinging them as they hopped in unison up the staircase.

9:02 a.m.

I LOVE YOU SO MUCH THAT IT HURTS TO BREATHE WHEN I LOOK AT you, Jade Pierce thought.

Her toddler son, Oliver, squirmed in his dad's long, strong arms. Brady Pierce's chuckle was deep and filled with the genuine pride a young father cannot hide when measuring the strength of his boy's grip on his own thumb.

If only Brady worshipped me, too, Jade thought sadly.

But she knew better now. He'd been just using her. As long as she did her part, as long as she played nice-nice with Bettina and the PHM&T committee, he'd allow her to stick around.

I could leave, she thought. *I should leave. But if I do, I'll never win him back.*

She knew her ex-husband lusted for her. She saw it in his eyes, which followed her whenever she entered the room. She made damn sure Brady found it hard to resist her.

Still, to her chagrin, he never initiated their lovemaking.

Except for one blissful night. On Christmas Eve, after she'd presented Brady with an album filled with photos of Oliver and his new toddler friends from the club, he'd been so touched by the gift that he not only took her into his arms, but welcomed her into his bed.

She had hoped—*prayed*—this meant he'd finally fallen in love with her.

But Brady's not-so-subtle looks of longing for Ally, whenever she was near, was obvious to Jade.

And those admiring glances broke her heart.

Despite the PHM&T application committee's attempts to pit all the probationary Onesies against each other, Jade felt she had bonded with Lorna, Jillian and Ally. That is, until she saw Ally turning impulsively to kiss Brady just as the clock struck midnight on New Year's Eve.

That vision was now scorched in Jade's memory.

Finally, Brady gets what he wants, Jade thought. *Playmates for our son.*

And one for himself.

Suddenly Brady glanced over at her. Did he notice the sadness in her eyes when she looked at him? Apparently not, because his gaze held no sympathy, only bemused annoyance. "Jade, hon, your cell phone has been buzzing for the past five minutes! Join the rest of us on planet Earth, okay?"

To rouse herself from her pity, Jade shrugged, then snapped open her phone. But before she had a chance to speak, the voice on the other end said, "Hey, sweet thang, so tell me, are you wearing panties?"

The question stunned her like a blow to the back of the head.

Of course she recognized the caller's voice. It had been haunting her since she saw him for the first time in over a year this past Halloween. It belonged to Bettina's husband, Art Connaught.

Thank God he hadn't remembered where he knew her from. That was because most of the time they'd been together, he'd only had eyes for her G-string-clad backside. Or he'd stare at her naked breasts, which jiggled as she worked her pole on the Condor Club's stage.

In truth, she barely remembered him, either. Like many of the club's patrons, he wasn't there to make eye contact, but to feel the dancers' soft, taunt skin against his lap. And to mutter shaming filth into her ear. Yes, that was her strongest memory of him.

The bouncers at the Condor Club were familiar with his dirty talk, too, which spewed its filth whenever they muscled him out of the club for breaking the strip joint's very clear rules: look, drool, tip, but don't touch.

It was obvious Art's memory had cleared by the night of the Cross's annual New Year's Eve party. He hadn't just whispered his typical trash in her ear that night, but also a threat: convince Brady to invest with him, or he'd tell Bettina about her past and ruin Oliver's chances of remaining in PHM&T.

"Ha ha! I know what you're thinking," Art murmured. "'How presumptuous of you, Art!' And you're right. Not to call, but to ask such an intimate question. But of course you're wearing panties! I guess what I should have asked is, are they crotchless or edible?"

Jillian turned her back to Brady and walked toward the living room's big picture window. Across the street, young couples in love strolled hand in hand on the path surrounding the lake in front of San Francisco's stately Palace of Fine Arts, where white swans glided across its tranquil surface.

Everyone is happy but me, Jade thought wistfully.

Then it struck her. *When it came to Brady, Oliver was still her trump card, Ally or no Ally.*

But if she got kicked out of the club, she'd lose both Brady and her son.

She couldn't let that happen.

Besides, Brady had to invest his money with someone. Why not Art? Maybe the fact that he was a ruthless son-of-a-bitch with no sense of morality was a big plus in the game of high finance.

In a sugar-sweet voice, she loudly proclaimed, "Bettina! So good to hear from you! …Yes, you caught us just in time. Brady and I were just about to take Oliver on a little stroll before getting ready for the PHM&T luncheon."

"So, good ol' Brady is standing there, eh?" Art drawled

from the phone. "Love it! Hey, how 'bout I talk dirty to you? Would that make you all hot and bothered? No? That's okay. We both know that's not why I'm calling. I'm just checking in to see if we're still on for a date."

Oh my God, he's much too loud, Jade thought.

She cupped the phone closer to her ear. "You're confirming that date to go out, the four of us? Yes, of course I remember." Out of the corner of her eye, she could see Brady mimicking a knife going across his throat. All she could do was shrug helplessly. "We discussed tomorrow, Saturday the twelfth, right? Sevenish?"

Brady groaned loudly. *Well, too bad.* She waved him away.

"That's a good girl." Art growled in her ear. "I'll tell my ol' lady I confirmed our little foursome. Why don't we say Ozumo on Steuart? I'll get us their little private room." He laughed heartily. "Damn, if only it *were* a private party, just you and me. Would you let me eat sushi off your bodacious bod? Ah well, I guess this is the next best thing. Just make sure Brady brings his checkbook with him. One way or another, he's picking up the tab, right? You've sucked on that tit before, so you know how sweet it is. Time to give the rest of us some time at that trough."

He hung up the phone before she could say anything.

Brady shook his head at her. "Damn, Jade, I thought I told you to get us out of that date. Bettina's husband made it clear at their New Year's Eve shindig that he wants me to invest in one of his funds, but no way that's going to happen. I'm already looking into Matt Connaught's startup lead, remember?"

She took Oliver from Brady's arms. "I still think we should hang out with Bettina and Art. You know, for Oliver's sake. And besides, you've got enough money that throwing a few thou Art's way shouldn't be such a big deal."

Brady shrugged. "After today, it'll be official. You and Oliver are in the club, so why should I?"

"Nothing is written in stone. Bettina and her posse are always looking for infractions. If you want to stay in the club, you can't even be separated. You know that." Rocking her son on her hip, she murmured, "Could you imagine what would happen if, say, she found out Ally still sits on the board of the company she started and is faking her marriage to that gay lawyer friend of hers?"

Brady looked at her suspiciously. "How would Bettina find that out?"

"Who knows? But hey, those kinds of things have a way of getting out." Jade smiled innocently. "I'm just pointing out that if we want to stay in the club, we *all* have to watch our P's and Q's."

Brady's frown was accompanied by a shrug. "That means you, too. Seriously, are you going to wear that blouse to the luncheon?"

Jade raised a brow. "Why? What's wrong with it?"

"For one thing, it's see-through. And for another, you're not wearing a bra."

Her smirk faded. "I thought you liked this blouse."

"I do. I just don't think Bettina will. But I'm guessing

Art will. Hey, here's a thought. Why don't you save it for our double date? Maybe he'll be so captivated by your headlights that he'll forget to ask for any of my money."

Go to hell, Jade thought.

She shot him the bird as she headed up the stairs.

But because she knew Brady was still watching her as she climbed the staircase with Oliver, she made sure to keep her shoulders back and hold her head high.

She also knew he got her message, loud and clear.

❦

SHE STILL SUSPECTS SOMETHING, BRADY THOUGHT. *AND IF SHE finds out she's right, she'll hurt Ally with what she knows.*

He could feel the color leaving his face.

I can't let her do that. No way in hell.

Since their kiss on New Year's Eve, Brady had called Ally's cell at least a half dozen times, but she never picked up. She may have admitted to him that she loved him, but she was still conflicted over her feelings.

He knew she truly liked Jade and didn't want to hurt her friend.

If Jade was the reason Ally got ousted from the club, she'd blame him. And she'd have every right to do so.

All the pieces of his grand scheme for Oliver had fallen into place. His son had been accepted to PHM&T. Bettina had taken Jade under her wing. Jade was finally acting like a real mother to her son...

For now, he warned himself. And only as long as I pretend I'm interested in her.

He could talk with Ally. He could laugh with her. In his opinion, she got everything about him: why he had been driven to make a success of himself, and then sell his company in order to focus on raising his child.

Because she had done exactly the same thing.

Jade would never understand him. God love the girl, in his opinion, she was clueless. This would never change.

At that moment, he made a vow to himself. *I can't let her stand in the way of my happiness.*

Sure, he'd have dinner with the Crosses, play up to Bettina, and string Art along.

Oliver's happiness didn't have to happen at his and Ally's expense no matter what cards Jade thought she had up her sleeve.

She rarely wore sleeves anyway.

Hell, she rarely wore a bra.

At least that was one thing he admired about her.

10:05 a.m.

"OH! YOU'RE BACK!" BARRY SIMON KISSED HIS BEST FRIEND, Ally Thornton, but the concern in his eyes undermined the surprised smile on his face.

"Yep, as promised, Friday morning. Sorry I'm late. The traffic coming up from Carmel was heavier than I anticipated." Ally looked beyond him into his living room. "Thanks so much for looking after Zoe these past couple of days. I really needed the time to think things through."

"What's a baby sperm donor-slash- daddy-slash- lawyer-slash- guardian-slash- BFF for, anyway?" He shrugged. "And besides, if you've finally come to your senses about this crush you've got on that married dude, it was worth it."

"Oh." Ally's smile faded. "About that. I'm sorta still on the fence."

Ally couldn't lie to Barry. The elation she'd felt when she kissed Brady at Bettina's New Year's Eve party had yet to fade. The two-day getaway to Carmel was supposed to clear her head on the issue, but it had the opposite effect. She was more confused than ever as to what she should do next.

Just minutes before the kiss, she'd made the perfect case to Brady as to why they shouldn't be anything other than friends. For example, the PHM&T applications committee presumed she was already married—to Barry, in fact. They also thought Brady was still married to his ex, Jade.

Front and center in her argument was her own relationship with Brady's ex. The challenging tasks given to her and the probationary members of PHM&T's Onesies group hadn't pitted them against each other. Instead, it brought them closer. She knew Jade was fighting hard to stay in her son's life, and she admired her for that.

And now that she knew the true circumstances of Jade and Brady's relationship, it was clear to Ally that Jade was doing everything she could to win back Brady's love.

But Brady wanted Ally. He had countered all of Ally's arguments—including her accusation that he only wanted her because it was a safe bet that she'd never give in—by asking her to allow herself the happiness she deserved.

There were too many reasons to say no, but one very important reason to say yes. No other man had been willing to take a chance on her.

He was begging to be that man.

Seeing Barry's frown, Ally quickly added, "Barry, please try to understand! I'm a single mom, closing in on forty. Whereas most of the men I meet resent my professional success, Brady loves and respects the fact that I built a company on my own, because he's done exactly the same thing. And while most men are intimidated by my financial freedom, Brady finds this a relief."

Barry laughed. "I'm sure he does! Arm charms are expensive."

Ally frowned. "That's another thing. He loves me, even though I don't look like... well you know—"

"Yeah, I know—a Playboy centerfold." Barry hesitated, then added, "Like Jade."

Yes, like Jade. Ally looked down at her breasts, which were not exactly small, and not exactly sagging, but they'd certainly never get her on the cover of *Esquire*, either.

When she looked up again, Barry was still scowling. Obviously, he was still worried for her. It was time to change the subject. She gave him a big sunny smile. "So, where's our little girl?"

"Christian took Zoe out to... Well, let's just say they're bonding. And the great news is that they should be back any moment." He looked down at his watch. "You said Bettina's 'you're now all my bitches' celebration is at noon, right? So, you've got plenty of time to get there. And then you've got the next four and a half years to regret putting yourself through it. Not to mention Zoe."

"Zoe is having a blast with all her little friends in the club."

"And you're having a blast with one of their fathers. It's only a matter of time before that little kewpie doll, Jade, finds out about you and her hubby." Barry's eyes rolled skyward. "You lied to get into this club. And now Brady has put you in a position where you'll have to lie to all these great friends you claimed to have made. Tell me. What's going to happen when they find out about the two of you? We both know it's inevitable." Despite his frown, he took her hand in his. "You know how I feel about the club. If you'd been axed, I'd be doing cartwheels. But to voluntarily leave it and all the friends you and Zoe have made, just because that *player* is making goo-goo eyes at you—" Barry took a deep breath. "Ally, he's a man with all the things that implies."

"You sound as if you know something about Brady that I don't."

Barry shrugged. "We men aren't always honest with those who love us. Especially when we know it knocks us off some imaginary pedestal."

It's sweet, the way he's so protective of me, Ally thought. *He may not know Brady the way I do, but he's got a point. Zoe comes first, always.*

So that Barry couldn't see her tears, she turned her head

toward the window. Thank goodness, Christian, Barry's partner, was pushing Zoe's carriage up the block.

"Look, Barry, I hear you. I'll let Brady know in no uncertain terms that we're just friends, and no more." She kissed his cheek and then put a smile on her face. "Christian's back —just in time to get Zoe ready. I bought her the cutest little dress for the ceremony."

"Um… Ally, about Zoe… There was a bit of an incident—"

"What? What do you mean, 'incident?'"

"Nothing too serious. We had her in the yard with us while Christian and I were weeding the flowerbeds, and… Well, while Christian and I weren't looking—"

At that moment, the door opened. Christian winced when he saw Ally. With an apologetic nod, he reached down to lift Zoe out of her stroller.

Ally stared down at her child. Except for her eyes, nose, and mouth, every inch of the little girl was wrapped in a sports bandage. Her nose had been patted down with a thick paste.

Ally kept a smile on her face as she picked up her squealing daughter and cooed. "Hi, sweetie! Mommy certainly missed you!" Turning back to the men, she hissed. "Oh my God! Can someone explain to me why my daughter looks like a mummy?"

"I was trying to explain that she fell into some poison sumac," Barry started.

"At first, we thought it was some of the New Zealand ivy we'd planted last year, so we didn't think much of it." Christian interjected. "She'd pulled it up by the roots and was running over with it. Just like a little pixie sprite! She was so adorable!"

"Yeah well, 'adorable' doesn't begin to describe her now, does it?" Ally grimaced.

"It happened overnight. I guess she scratched open a lot of those odious little pimples." Barry shuddered. "We thought it best that Christian take her to the pediatrician as soon as possible."

I guess so that I wouldn't murder him in front of my child, Ally thought. "What's that stuff on her nose?"

"Some homeopathic cream. The doctor recommended it —although I think the green color makes her look like a tiny version of the Wicked Witch of the West," Christian explained. "And it's all over her body and her face, too. The bandages keep her from rubbing it off. He says the swelling will be gone in a couple of days."

"Yeah, well, that won't work. She's got the club's induction ceremony today! I can't take her looking like this!"

Barry grinned mischievously. "So miss it."

Ally glared back at him. "Not on your life." She grabbed her daughter and her bags, and headed out the door. "Thanks. For... whatever."

Barry winced. "You don't have to say it, really. I mean, what are friends for?"

Ally glowered back. "When I figure it out, you'll be the first to know."

She slammed the door behind her.

10:15 a.m.

LIKE MOST BOLINAS, CALIFORNIA NATIVES, LORNA FIGURED OUT early in life that the best time of year to venture out on the tiny coastal burg's infamous nude beach was in January, when the brisk, frigid air ensured that only a few brave souls were exposing themselves.

She averted her eyes from any flesh that was goose-pimply, shriveled, perky, or standing at attention, all the while wishing those around her had the good graces to give her the same courtesy. But no. Since Lorna was fully clothed, she was indeed an oddity to be stared at.

She was also a stranger, which was rare in a town where the inhabitants tore down state road signs so no outsiders could find their little coastal village. This had been the case since the '70s, when Bolinas became a haven for hippies looking to trade the hustle, hassle and fog of San Francisco for the rolling mist-kissed cliffs, crashing surf, and secluded beaches of this tiny live-and-let-live town.

Truth be known, she was wearing the same sleek Michael Kors print jeans and form-fitting Dolce & Gabbana blazer since Tuesday afternoon, when she left Dante in Matthew's arms.

It had taken her ninety minutes to drive up the coast. But it had taken her two nights to get the nerve to walk down to the beach.

She spent those evenings in a hotel room above a local hangout called Smiley's Schooner Saloon. While some blue-grass bandleader wailed about lost love and dark roads under full moons, she worked on her computer, pulling up every bit of research she could find regarding genetic tracers for autism. By doing so, she could see why Matthew would question her, why he would seek to find the answer to the cause of his son's diagnosis.

She couldn't blame him. If the shoe were on the other foot, she'd be doing the same.

The rest of her time was spent pacing the threadbare carpet as she practiced what she would say to the one person she knew could assuage her guilt about Dante's condition:

Her mother.

But the time of reckoning had come. It was now or never, if she were to get home in time to attend the PHM&T club celebratory luncheon.

If she wanted to save her marriage.

And if she wanted to save her son from a lifetime of misunderstanding and cruelty.

The gray, wet sand seeped and sifted through her open-toed Kate Spade pumps as she marched down the beach toward the lagoon that separated Bolinas' beach from the long, slim spit that was the tail end of Stinson, the beach for Bolinas' neighboring town.

Although she wore large sunglasses, she held up a palm to ward off the warm rays emanating from the still low sun in the east, scanning the dunes until she found what she was looking for: a large red tent. From its peaked roof, a triangular flag adorned with the image of eight Roman goddesses of fertility or childbirth—Bona Dea, Candelifera, Carmenta,

Fecunditas, Feronia, Libera, Lucinda and Juno—snapped crisply in the wind.

As she made her way over, she repeated to herself, *I can do this… I can do this… I can do this…. for Dante.*

When she finally reached the door of the tent, she smacked it gently a few times. "Hera? Hera, are you there? It's me… Lorna."

At first, she heard nothing. Then there was rustling inside the tent and loud whispers. A moment later two heads popped out from behind the tent's flap. They belonged to women—twins, in fact. They were pop-eyed, all smiles, and in their late fifties. Their hair, more zinc now in color than what once was a bright copper hue, was long and wavy.

"Are you her?" one asked.

Lorna paused before answering. It had been years since she'd seen her mother. But knowing the woman who had birthed her as well as she did, there was certainly reason to believe it was a loaded question in more ways than one.

"If you're asking me if I'm Hera's daughter, then… Yes, I am."

There. She said it out loud. She couldn't remember the last time she'd done that.

They stared at her as if she were an apparition. Finally, a voice from within the tent said, "Let her enter."

The women beckoned her in.

Aw hell, there's no turning back now, Lorna thought.

⁊

THE TENT WAS LARGE ENOUGH TO HOLD TEN. ALL WERE WOMEN. Most were naked, pregnant, and chanting with their eyes closed. One of the twins whispered, "Silence, please! We're in the middle of a pre-birth Wiccan ceremony!"

Workshops and Wiccan ceremonies were how her mother made her living. *Well,* Lorna thought, *everyone has to put food on the table somehow.*

The twins led Lorna behind a sheer curtain in the back of the tent. It took a while for her eyes to adjust before she made out her mother: Hera Harmony. The older woman sat in front of a stone altar adorned with seashells, herbs, and sand dollars. Acknowledging Lorna with a nod, she then rose gracefully off her haunches. Chimes tinkled as she moved, barefoot, toward her daughter.

When finally they were face-to-face, Lorna hesitated at first, but then she put her arms around her mother.

Hera stood there, motionless.

Well, what did I expect? Lorna chided herself silently.

Her mother was just as she remembered her: slim and deliberate, bright blue eyes wide and alert. It had been nearly a decade. So yes, there were some physical changes. Long lines were clearly etched in her forehead and around her mouth. Her hair, cropped gamine short, was now almost completely white.

And she still did not approve of Lorna's choices.

This was evident in her very first question to her daughter: "Do you know how many Chinese orphans will be crippled, blinded, or beaten in the making of that designer dreck you're wearing?"

Lorna sighed. "No. But I've no doubt you do, and that you're now going to tell me."

"Most are teenagers or younger. They work in abysmal conditions, and are paid only a quarter of what they need to survive. Whatever meager wages they do make, seventy-five percent of it goes to feed themselves and their families. Now, aren't you ashamed of yourself?"

"Hera, I came to tell you that I'm married."

"Ah!" Hera's eyes widened as she took in this news. "I guess congratulations are in order. What is your bride's name?"

Lorna stifled another sigh. "Matthew. Sorry to disappoint you, but I married a man."

Hera rolled her eyes. "I guess we are who we are." She shrugged. "So tell me, who are you now?"

Lorna knew Hera could not care less that she graduated cum laude from Berkeley. If she had, she would've come when Lorna invited her to the graduation. And her mother certainly didn't want to hear about their home on Russian Hill or that she drove a gas-guzzling SUV.

Instead, she gave the answer she knew her mother was looking for. "I am a satisfied being."

Hera arched a brow. "Merely 'satisfied?' Not blissful?"

Lorna closed her eyes. *Why must she always judge me? Why does she parse my words? Does she want me to be happy?* Lorna wondered. *Don't all mothers want that for their children? Or is it that they want their children to need them, always and forever?*

Dante would always need her; she knew that now. He would never know the kind of independence she'd had, both growing up with a mother who had raised her not to depend on anyone and an absentee father. For that, she felt sorry for her son.

On the other hand, Dante's condition would be the true test of her love for him. She planned on living up to the challenge.

She was relieved her mother had never been tested the same way. Her guess is that Hera would've failed miserably. She'd always made Lorna feel like a burden, her cross to bear. Her Earth Mother principles were great in theory, but never in practice.

Hera is right in one regard, Lorna thought. *We are who we are.*

She had one favor of Hera. Hopefully, this one time she wouldn't fail Lorna. "Hera, I'd like you to meet Matt. And also our son, Dante."

Hera blinked. "Oh! A *son?*"

"Yes," Lorna declared firmly. "He's going on twenty months. I want you to be a part of his life. He'll need all of us."

Her mother tilted her head. "Why is that?"

"Dante's been diagnosed with autism." Lorna bowed her head. "The doctor is running tests. We're doing everything we can to nurture him, but it will be an uphill battle." She hesitated. "There are some theories that the condition may be genetic."

Hera rolled her eyes. "You're wrong. Do you feed him foods with gluten? And I'll bet you vaccinated him. Am I right? Ha! I thought so! Have you checked his mercury level? I'm guessing it's sky high. By the way, I know a shaman who does healing work in this area—"

"Hera, no, please! No shamans! Let's just..." Lorna clenched her fists at her side. "I'd rather the doctor take the lead on this. All I'm asking of you is to meet my husband and your grandson, and to give me your moral support."

"'Nutty New Age theories?'" Hera pursed her thin lips. Finally, she nodded. "Okay, Lorna. Just tell me what you want me to do."

Lorna's hand shook as she opened her purse and pulled out a sheet of paper. "Here's my telephone number and address. Perhaps you can come over, say, next Thursday, in the afternoon? And... I hate to ask, but since we're looking into all sorts of causes for Dante's condition, perhaps you'd be willing to give a DNA sample? There is this theory that it could be genetic chromosomal damage. If that's the case—"

Hera shook her head. "If that's the case, it's too late to do anything about it now."

Lorna knew she was right. Nothing would change Dante's situation.

But the more love and support he has, the better his future would be. *Here is Hera's opportunity to be a part of it,* she thought.

"It was stupid of me to ask. Forget I brought it up. In any case, I look forward to you meeting them on Thursday. That is, if you still want to come."

Hera smiled. "I wouldn't miss it for the world."

What have I gotten myself into? Lorna thought.

She turned to leave, then remembered the last question she had for her mother.

"Hera, where is Peter nowadays?"

Hera laughed. "Peter? Oh my goddess, he could be anywhere! Last I heard, he was down in Costa Rica. No, wait... Venice Beach. If you still feel the need to find the weakest link, your father certainly fits the bill. We both know it." Hera shrugged. "Lorna, Fate has played its hand. As for blame, there's always enough of it to go around."

❧

LORNA MADE IT BACK TO THE HOUSE JUST A FEW MINUTES before noon. She was frantic. If Matt hadn't gotten her text or hadn't heeded it, she'd be rushing to get Dante into something decent. Having been gone for two days, she was sure the laundry was sky high with his dirty toddler togs.

As it turned out, Matt was sitting on the front stoop with Dante in his lap. Their toddler was dressed in the little tuxedo she'd bought for him back before Labor Day when she'd received the notice of her probationary acceptance to the PHM&T.

When she got out of the car, Matt stood up. "We're glad you're home," was all he said, but he wasn't smiling as he handed Dante over to her.

Seeing the astonished look on her face, Matt said, "Now that he's officially in the club, he should dress the part."

She nodded gratefully. "I appreciate you doing all this.

I'm not saying that your suggestion last time of the track suit was off base or anything—"

"You didn't have to say it. I overheard Bettina's sarcastic jokes about it at Mother's house." He shrugged. "His future will be filled with people looking to poke holes in his happiness. He doesn't need any help from his idiot father."

Tenderly, she touched Matt's cheek. "Matt, please don't call yourself an idiot. You're one of the smartest men I know. And one of the sweetest."

He took her in his arms and kissed her, long and hard.

When, finally, they parted, they were both crying. He raised his eyes so they'd meet hers. "I'll always be right here for you, Lorna. And I'll be here for Dante, too." His smile was bittersweet. "Did you find what you were looking for?"

She nodded. "I owed it to my mother to ask her to meet my family—you and Dante—in person. Hera is looking forward to it. She'll be here next Thursday. I'm sure she'll be open to answering any questions you may have about me. And also about her and… my father. Of course, Hera doesn't know where he is. For now, that may be for the best."

She buried her head in Dante's back. The sweet scent of baby powder and lotion revived her and gave her the resolve she needed to add, "Matt, I started out by asking her for a DNA sample. But I didn't press the issue. What's the point? Do we need to have someone to blame? It won't change anything."

He shrugged. "I know. I was acting like a jerk. It's just that I feel so—so *hopeless*."

"I do too. We just have to take this one day at a time."

"I'm glad you feel that way. In fact, I'm hoping you'll agree to go with me to a marriage counselor. We both need reassurance that…that we're in this together."

She nodded slowly. "Yes, of course."

"Good." He seemed relieved. "And I want to be with Dante during all his tests. I've also set up bi-weekly appointments with a physical therapist whose specialty is autistic infants—of course, on the days he's not hanging with his PHM&T buds."

She rewarded his declaration with a teary smile.

Matt looked away. "Lorna, I haven't mentioned Dante's condition yet, to anyone."

Lorna knew he was referring to Eleanor and Bettina. "I understand. In fact, I'm glad you'll be meeting Hera without any other family distractions."

He laughed. "Yeah, in this case, the more does not equal 'the merrier.'" He kissed her forehead. "You'd better go shower and change your clothes. Whatever fresh hell Bettina has in store for you and your pals will seem less devious if you're in one of your killer designer dresses."

She laughed. He was right. And he knew her so well.

It was great to be home.

Even Bettina couldn't ruin that for her.

12:20 p.m.

THIS IS MY FIEFDOM, BETTINA THOUGHT AS SHE GAZED PROUDLY at all the other mothers who were gliding toward their assigned seats at the annual Pacific Heights Moms & Tots Club New Year's Kick-Off Luncheon held as always at the St. Francis Yacht Club.

Bettina's great-grandfather had been one of its founding members. Without hesitation, the club's directors did what they could to accommodate her whims for making the event perfect. The dining room, which had an incomparable panoramic view of the Golden Gate Bridge, was laid out with five circular tables that sat ten, the number of mothers in each of the age-specific groups within the club. Beside place cards, one of two floral themes graced each place setting: pink (with pink rose buds) or blue (with hydrangeas of that hue), depending on the sex of the child whose mother was to sit there.

This particular gathering would also introduce the four probationary Onesies applicants who, after several months of highly competitive challenges, won full membership in the Pacific Heights Moms & Tots Club. Having read Bettina's veiled threat in the carefully worded invitation, which stated "Your presence to this event is appreciated on or before eleven forty-five a.m.," many PHM&T members and their fidgety offspring had lined up outside the yacht club's double doors as early as eleven.

"They must think Apple is here to unveil another damn iPhone," the doorman muttered under his breath as he peered out at the growing crowd.

The early birds included the six legacy Onesies moms: Hillary Trumbull and her daughter, Ava; Marcia Broderick and her daughter, Ella; Bella Adams with her son, Liam;

Doreen Landau and her son, Ethan; Janine Ledbetter and her son, Jackson; and Gwen Markham and her son, Nathan. All already had a child in one of the other age groups.

By eleven thirty, all the members were seated, and their children were already ensconced in the adjacent "children's party room" where healthy snacks had been set up and twelve of the city's most highly regarded sitters were standing by to feed, diaper, and play age-appropriate games.

Excitement was already crackling through the air.

Perfect, Bettina thought. *Now as each of the winners arrive, I'll walk her in and personally reintroduce her to the club.*

The first probationer to come in was Lorna with Dante in tow. Bettina grimaced. Too bad it wasn't one of the other winners. Her ears pricked up, alert to any faint murmurs of nepotism. She need not worry. The emotional choke collar around her members' necks was always held tight within her slim fingers. No one wanted to be yanked onto the carpet, let alone exiled from the club for grousing about their fearless founder.

"You're prompt. How refreshing," Bettina murmured in Lorna's ear as she air-kissed her sister-in-law and patted her solemn little nephew on his check. Then she shuttled Lorna into the dining room and announced in a loud voice, "Ladies, your attention! The first of our newest members has arrived. Please welcome Lorna Connaught, who brought the revenue to our recipe book fundraiser to Olympian heights!"

The applause was enthusiastic. Too much so for Bettina's liking. She nodded at Mallory Wickett, who took the hint and practically shoved Lorna in the direction of her assigned table.

Just at that moment, Jade walked in, holding Oliver. Bettina's eyes swept over her appraisingly. "Ah, and here is another of our newest members, Jade Pierce." She held out her hand to Jade, who took it hesitantly. "Such a fashion plate! Is that Valentino? ...I thought so. Black lace over white poplin and buttoned to the collar! So innocently school-girl-ish! You carry it off *soooo* well. And such a wonderful addition to our club! We'll never forget your pumpkin patch event." She turned toward the other mothers. "Am I right, ladies?"

At this last declaration, the thunderous applause over Jade's choice of couture diminished to a few timid claps. The memory of Lily's plaintive screams in the corn maze was still fresh in every young mother's mind.

By the way Jade scurried to her seat, she'd never forget the incident either. Or maybe she was afraid Bettina might change her mind about her membership.

I want her to be afraid, Bettina thought. *Very afraid. Anything to keep her in line. At least until Art is managing Brady's portfolio.*

Jillian's entry into the dining room was somewhat disconcerting. From what Bettina could see, the poor thing was sweating right through her coat, and her shoes were inexplicably mud-spattered. Obviously, she hadn't driven or arrived in a hired car. Bettina had heard that Jillian was an avid jogger, but this was ridiculous. No one jogged in Louboutins. Heck, you could barely walk in them.

Noting Bettina's disapproval, Jillian cast her eyes downward.

Bettina shrugged. "Well, well, just in time! Here is our third new member, Jillian Frederickson, and her twin daughters, Addison and Amelia." She signaled one of the sitters to wheel the girls' stroller into the playroom. Turning back to Jillian, she added, "My dear, I think I gained five pounds just sniffing the delicious pies you brought to our after-Thanksgiving potluck! And my favorite event this year was our holiday party. Wouldn't you agree, Mallory?"

There were a few audible groans at the memory of Mallory's feisty little brat, Angus, pulling down the witch's cap on top of the Fairmont Hotel's gingerbread house.

Mallory rarely smiled, so no one was surprised that she wasn't doing so now. And when Jillian yelped as Mallory pushed her into her seat, no one batted an eye, either.

Bettina shrugged. Even Mallory couldn't ruin her day. This morning she'd finally received a text from the Tibetan mastiff breeder. Since leaving Le Marcel Bakery, she had emailed the breeder every hour on the hour. Finally, just this morning, the damn woman emailed back! Her response was short and to the point. *Come by at four o'clock, sharp, next Tuesday. I live in St. Francis Wood. My address is -….*

No way in hell was Bettina going to miss that date! And she'd take Lily with her to pick out the puppy herself. It was the least she could do. The lost ballet skirts had upset her little daughter to no end. "Ballet Master will make me wear pink," she wailed. "I'll be humiliated!"

In truth, even the promise of a new puppy brought only a

half-hearted shrug. But Bettina knew once Lily saw the puppy, held it in her arms, and trained it to obey her and to love her, everything would change.

Yes, obedience is the key to every relationship, she thought.

At that moment, Ally walked in. "Finally!" Bettina smiled over at her. "Last but not least, we have Ally Thornton, and…and…"

She stared at the package in Ally's arms. Was it a child? By the way the thing was wrapped, for all she knew it could have been a *Dia de los Muertos* figurine.

Bettina frowned. "I *presume* this is little Zoe."

Ally blushed, but nodded just the same. "So sorry we're late! Zoe just got back from the doctor. That's why she's wrapped up this way—to keep from scratching and spreading it around—"

"Oh my God! She's got measles!" cried one mother who was sitting at the Foursies table. She vaulted toward the playroom. "Sadie has never been exposed! I've got to get her out of here, or they won't let us make our flight for Europe the day after tomorrow!"

"No, no! It's got to be mumps," a mother at the Twosies table screamed. "And there are so many babies here who haven't finished their shot sequences—including my Zachary!"

She popped up so fast that she took the tablecloth with her. All the vases on the table fell over. Their contents of flowers and water washed into the laps of other mothers sitting with her, who squealed in dismay.

A woman from the Threesies table stood up and pointed

at Ally. "Did you say your child wasn't vaccinated—and that she has Rubella? How could you expose our children to her? How could you?"

"Wait! I didn't say she had any of those things! And she's certainly not contagious! My goodness, *it's only poison sumac!*"

Too late. The stampede toward the playroom sounded like an 8.0 earthquake.

Bettina clicked her knife against her Baccarat glass goblet. "Ladies, please....PLEASE! SIT DOWN!"

Everyone froze. Glances were exchanged. Did they dare disobey?

Of course not.

Slowly, they made their way back to their seats.

Bettina glared at Ally. "You did an excellent job with the adult holiday party, but let's face it, it was a snore. That said, I never expected this kind of drama from you. And isn't your husband a doctor?"

The question took Ally by surprise. "Um... Barry? No! He's is a lawyer."

Damn! Well, that certainly presents a vexing dilemma, Bettina thought. If she axed Ally for bringing a child who wasn't contagious to a meeting, she might be facing a lawsuit, and that would never do. Better she should hold her powder. Besides, of all the women in the Onesies, even Bettina had to concede that Ally was the most likable.

Which brought her to the task at hand, finding the best Onesies mother to join her and the other she'd considered the most worthy—or at least the most malleable—on the Top Moms Application Committee.

In her opinion, the pickings were slim to none. Had any of the legacies been worthy, they'd already be sitting on the committee. At best they were weak Plan Bs. Still, they too would be put through their paces along with Those Formerly Known as Onesies Probies.

She smiled down on them grandly from the podium. "Ladies, now that I have your full attention, I'm letting you in on a momentous change to our club's bylaws. From now on, the newest member of PHM&T's Top Moms Application Committee—that is, the mother who'll join us from the Onesies Group—will rise from the ashes of her fellow group members' failed tasks, like the fabled phoenix."

Bettina paused so that her oratorical eloquence could be duly appreciated.

From the blank stares of the others in the room, her pause had given everyone else a reason to scratch their beautifully coiffed heads.

Bettina sighed loudly. "Seriously? Okay, this isn't rocket science, so try to follow." She reached into the podium and pulled out a tiny glass heart-shaped candy dish filled with folded tabs.

In unison, Lorna, Jillian, Ally and Jade also sighed loudly and resignedly. They'd recognize it anywhere. The challenge tasks they'd pulled from the thick-sided, diamond-etched Baccarat bric-a-brac had been the bane of their existences these past few months.

Bettina ignored them. "I'll be asking all ten of the Onesies moms to pull a folded tab from this dish. Written on it is a challenge task. Between now and Mother's Day—quite appropriately, wouldn't you say?—these tasks will be completed. The current committee will judge who has excelled at it. And this woman—this *mother*—will be invited to join the committee."

The loudest gasps came from the Legacy Onesies' mothers. Whereas they'd enjoyed the trials and tribulations of the probationers, they never dreamed they'd be submitted to it themselves! But what choice did they have?

None, if they wanted to stay in the club.

They bowed their heads in shame.

"Okay now, who will go first?" Bettina asked brightly.

No one moved.

Annoyed, Bettina handed the dish to Kimberley Savitch and waved her hand toward the Onesies table. "Pass it around."

Smiling slyly, Kimberley placed it in front of Jade.

Jade stared at it for an eternity before closing her eyes and plucking out a tab. Then, opening one eye, she read, "'Come up with an advanced placement class for the Fivesies.'" She stared at Bettina. "What does that mean?"

"Lucky you!" Bettina clasped her hands together in mock joy. "It should be both fun and easy! So that we can best prepare our little geniuses for their future academic experiences, we'll be giving them a much-needed head start by developing the kinds of advance placement classes we'd like to see in our schools. In fact, six others will get similar tasks. Another mom will also curate a Fivesies AP program, while two others will do so for the Foursies, and then one each for the Threesies, Twosies, and Onesies."

The women shifted in their seats uncomfortably. Seeing this, Bettina shrugged. "Not to worry! You'll have plenty of time to put together a curriculum outline and find an instructor with a stellar *curriculum vitae*. These are due no later than the Monday after Mother's Day. Interviews will commence the following Wednesday. Should your class be accepted, these forty-five-minute classes will begin the Wednesday after, and continue every Wednesday, through August. To make your group's Top Mom, you'll be judged on the class's originality, and the instructor's stellar credentials. Okay, next in line, please!"

It was Gwen Markham's turn. Her hand shook as it pulled out a tag. She frowned. "I've got to come up with a Foursies AP class."

"We'll alert the media, Gwen. Okay, Jillian, it seems you're next."

Jillian bit her lower lip, then reached into the dish. She sighed with relief. "I have the children's Valentine party."

Both Hillary Trumbull and Maureen Landau pulled Advanced Placement class coordination for the Twosies and Onesies respectively.

It was Lorna's turn. She pulled "Easter Egg Hunt Extravaganza" as her task.

Seeing Lorna's dismay, Bettina's lips curdled into a smirk. "Wonderful! I can't think of a better person to coordinate the dyeing, decorating and hiding of a thousand eggs in Lafayette Park!"

Ally smiled gaily when she saw her task. "I have the parent's Valentine party."

Bettina shrugged. "If you do it at your place, hold it inside, okay? Less chance of a poison sumac outbreak."

To their dismay, Marcia Broderick and Bella Adams were to create appropriately challenging advanced placement classes for the Threesies and Foursies respectively. Jane Ledbetter pulled the final AP class, for the Fivesies.

"May the odds be ever in your favor!" To express her jubilation, Bettina threw her well-toned arms in the air. "I'm famished! Shall we eat?"

She was not at all surprised that the ten Onesies moms barely ate their lunches.

They seemed to have lost their appetites.

2:15 p.m.

"HEY, SO LISTEN, I'VE GOT A PLAN!" ALLY RAN TO CATCH UP TO Jillian, who had been the first to vault out of the yacht club while the other mothers lingered leisurely to gossip and set up play dates.

"Great, because I need one. I'm at my wit's end." Jillian blinked away her tears. "I hate to say it out loud, but I'm desperately short on money."

Ally patted her friend's arm. "Let me walk you to your car."

Jillian blushed. "You can't. I no longer own one. It was repossessed this morning."

"Wow! I'm sorry, Jill. Hey, jump in with Zoe and me. I'll treat you and the girls to coffee at the Grove. And a piece of pie. Of course, it won't be half as delicious as yours."

Jillian laughed. "Stop it. You're embarrassing me. Besides, you had me at 'treat.'"

Ally waited with the twins until Jillian climbed into the backseat, then handed them to their mother before folding their stroller into the trunk of her BMW X6 SUV.

The moment she closed the hatch, her cell phone buzzed. She glanced down at it. There was a text from Brady.

When are we going to talk?

She groaned out loud.

"A problem?" The concern in Jillian's voice was touching.

Ally waved her hand dismissively. "Nothing that can't wait." She forced a smile on her face. "Shall we?"

🙚

IT TOOK ALLY AN HOUR TO LAY OUT HER BUSINESS PLAN TO Jillian, how she wanted to partner with her on a retail pie store, located somewhere in Pacific Heights or the Marina.

"Your pies are going to be even hotter than the cupcake craze." Ally was smiling, but the tone of her voice was all business. "I feel it in my heart, Jillian. It's the same feeling I got when I started Foot Fetish."

"I appreciate your belief in me, Ally. Really I do. And you know it couldn't come at a better time for me, what with the divorce and all." Jillian wiped away a tear. "But running a retail business takes a lot of time, not to mention money."

"We'll hire staff to manage the store on a day-to-day basis. And I'll do my voodoo: brand the store and do the marketing and promotion." She looked Jillian in the eye. "And, of course, I'll secure the financing, too. If our model works, we'll duplicate it in other locations in the city, and other cities around the country. Perhaps even go international with it." Ally leaned in close. "All you have to do is to come up with a few scrumptious pie recipes and bake the pies. Initially, of course. You'll supervise the baking when we get to the point where we need an industrial kitchen and baking staff."

Jillian couldn't believe her ears. Then a thought made her smile waver. "But—what if Bettina finds out?"

"Barry will make sure our corporation is veiled. By the time we go public, the kids will be in elementary school." Ally smiled. "We'll each be fifty-fifty partners, but any investor will want some equity stake, so we'll have to both peel off percentage points for that. Whatever it is, we hold onto a combined fifty-one percent. So, what do you say? Are you in?"

"Oh my God, of course!" Jillian jumped up and hugged her friend. "I can't believe this! It's a dream come true."

"Now the big question: what do you want to call it?"

Jillian thought for a moment. "What do you think about 'Life of Pie'?"

Ally laughed. "It's simple, to the point, and already familiar. Works for me."

To seal the deal, they toasted with their coffee mugs. But

their sips were interrupted by the buzz of Ally's cell phone. She glanced down, seeing a text from Brady.

Pretty please, with sugar on top?

She sighed, then texted back.

Tuesday afternoon. 5:30. Allyne Park, in Cow Hollow.

That would give her a few days to consider what to say to him.

Whatever it was, it would cost her something: a friendship and her support system or a chance at love. Which was worse?

She sighed. "A piece of pie sounds great right about now, but the Grove's can't compete with yours."

"If you and your little mummy give me a ride home, I'll whip one right up. Apple! You can take it home with you."

"Perfect. In exchange, I'm giving you an advance on your salary. Will six thousand cover you while you research our pie products?"

When Jillian squealed, heads from all over the coffee shop turned around to see what was causing the commotion. Embarrassed, she whispered, "I can't wait to get home and try out a few recipes. Ally, I can't thank you enough. And I won't let you down. Ever. You're a true friend."

Ally desperately needed to hear that, now more than ever.

CHAPTER FOUR

Tuesday, 8 January
9:10 a.m.

"It's been a whole week! Why haven't you returned my calls?" Art knew he sounded like a desperate fool, but he didn't care.

He missed Kelly.

Okay, in truth, he missed their sadistic sexcapades. That girl certainly knew how to wield a paddle.

Maybe she considered ignoring his calls as some form of foreplay. He viewed it as torture, which is why he begged. "Can we meet tomorrow? If that doesn't work, what about the day after? I'm flexible, if Friday works better."

Kelly's tone reeked of venomous scorn. "This is a joke, right?"

"A...what? Why would you say that?"

Kelly snickered. "Maybe you should ask your wife."

Art could feel the blood leaving his face. Suddenly his heart was racing. He tried to loosen his tie before he suffocated. "What the hell does Bettina have to do with us?"

"You mean she hasn't told you? Why, your bitch of a wife is onto you, my naughty little boy! She saw us on New Year's Eve. Yep, that's right! And guess what? *She has your favorite paddle.* When she confronted me, I gave it to her as a gift." Kelly's laugh's sent a chill go up Art's spine. "So, if I were you, I'd beg for mercy. Oops! I forgot we're talking about Bettina. No hope there."

The cell phone had been buzzing for two minutes or longer before his shaking hand was capable of hitting the off button. His mind was racing. If Bettina knew, why hadn't she said something?

He knew his wife too well to think she'd ever let bygones be bygones. She was biding her time until he screwed something up.

Like hooking Brady Pierce as an investment client.

That's it, he reasoned. *She wants to make sure we present a united front to the Pierces. If I blow it, she'll divorce me for sure now that she knows I've done it with her oldest, "dearest" friend.*

The thought that Bettina now had his favorite paddle made him shiver. Would she dare threaten to use it on him?

That would be sick.

Or maybe...

Maybe it would be *fun.*

For a fleeting moment, Art Cross contemplated the consequences of screwing up. He heard Bettina's voice commanding him to bend over the round tufted ottoman in their bedroom. He contemplated how she'd position herself over his naked ass. Would she angle her arm so that the paddle swatted him low and slow, or hard and fast?

His hands fell into his lap as his mind's eye played with both visions, one right after another, over and over again...

And again...

Until his assistant buzzed him, to tell him there was a client waiting in the lobby. He groaned. There was no way he could walk out there. Not with this humongous tent in his pants.

Maybe Bettina knowing his little secret wasn't so bad after all.

Well, tonight, he'd make it a point to find out.

11:44 a.m.

"THE BOSS WILL SEE YOU NOW," said JEN, ALLY'S ASSISTANT.

Ally winced. "Since when is Ellis Conway *my* boss?"

Jen pursed her lips. "Sorry, Ally! Honestly, it was a slip of the tongue. Of course, he's not *your* boss." She blushed. "It's just that... Well, I'm feeling a bit stressed right now, what with you working just part-time, and with all the layoffs going on around here. Did you know they've got me doubling as his assistant, too?"

"You're kidding!" Ally shook her head, confused. "What layoffs?"

"A third of the customer service staff and half of Foot

Fetish's warehouse personnel got laid off just after Christmas." Jen frowned. "Didn't you get the memo?"

"Apparently not." Ally felt guilty. No, make that angry. Was Ellis purposefully keeping her out of the loop?

She had started the company. When she sold it to Bracknell Industries, the corporation's board insisted she be part of the package. She agreed to do so, but only part time, now that Zoe was the single most important part of her life. One of Bracknell's rising stars, Ellis Conway, had come onboard to run the day-to-day operations.

Suddenly the idea of asking him to advocate Bracknell's investment in her pie shop proposal seemed futile.

But Ally's trump card was her knowledge that her continued role in Foot Fetish was integral to its financial success. She was its tastemaker. She was the one with the connection with footwear designers. As recent as last quarter, sales had been doing better than their CFO's projections. How had things come off the rails the past few weeks, and during their busiest season no less?

That was the first question she asked Ellis.

He swatted away her concern. "Ally, you're over-reacting. It's got nothing to do with you, believe me."

"You're wrong. Everything about this company has to do with me. Including the layoffs which, by the way, no one informed me were about to take place, nor any explanation as to why they were necessary!"

"That's quite a presumptuous statement for a part-time employee who would prefer to be a full-time mommy, isn't it?"

She wanted to slap the smirk off Ellis' face. To keep her cool, she murmured, "Unless she's the founder of the company, and she still sits on its board. So tell me. Why are you fucking up so badly?"

Ellis blanched at her question. "I'm not. It has nothing to do with me. I'm just following orders. The Bracknell men's apparel division has a large customer support staff. Why duplicate efforts here when we can lateral the calls there?" He shrugged. "The same thing goes for our warehouse facilities. Corporate already has it covered. We're just cutting out service redundancies."

"But shoes are something women find personal. Customer support has to be trained to best explain their advantages! And my warehouse guys were handpicked because they were quick and efficient."

Ellis put his hand on Ally's shoulder. She tried not to shudder, but she couldn't help it.

Feeling it, he frowned and pulled away.

Damn it, she thought. *I've blown it. Now Ellis won't give my pie shop proposal a second glance.*

"Your renewed commitment is refreshing," he said icily. "In fact, word from above is that we'll be expanding Bracknell's corporate board. If you want to suggest a candidate, Mr. Bracknell is all ears. Then again, I doubt your mommy duties have allowed you to rub shoulders with anyone with the biz chops to make the list."

"As a matter of fact, I could recommend Brady Pierce, if you want. He is—I mean, he and his wife are dear friends."

She regretted the retort even as the words left her mouth.

What the hell was she thinking? If Brady sat on the board with her, it would be more difficult than ever to be simply friends.

Friends. Really, could they ever be just that?

Who am I kidding, she wondered.

"You know *the* Brady Pierce?" Ellis's eyes glimmered with new respect for her. "Well, well, well! I'll certainly pass that tidbit to Mr. Bracknell. Now, what was it you needed from me?"

Ally shrugged nonchalantly, but her heart was racing. For once, she might actually have Ellis on her side. She smiled up at him. "I've put together a prospectus on a new business, something Bracknell may want to get in on the ground floor." She handed him the prospectus folder for *Life of Pie.*

"A pie shop?" He raised a brow.

"Really, it's the prototype for a bakery chain, with pie as its focus. Haven't you heard? Pie is the new cupcake. My research bears out its potential."

He smiled. "Hmmm. Intriguing. I'll be sure to pass it upstairs." Without further ado, he shut his door. But through the glass wall, she noticed he'd already opened the file.

At least, he's reading it, Ally thought.

She didn't know what made her more excited, the thought the Bracknell would finance the pie business, or that she and Brady might have a good excuse for seeing each other on a regular basis.

Just as friends, of course.

As if.

4:00 p.m.

THE MOMENT BETTINA SAW CALIGULA'S BITCH, ZENOBIA, IT WAS love at first sight.

Granted, the Tibetan mastiff's swollen belly —not to mention her painful panting, groaning, and farting— did little to reinforce the nobility of Zenobia's bloodline.

Bettina was willing to look beyond these temporary trifles. After all, the dog had been best of breed and best of show, a prizewinner many times over. The pick of Zenobia's litter would be a worthy addition of the Connaught-Cross household.

Sybil Vidal, Zenobia's owner, was a six-foot-two-inch redheaded giant. She laughed raucously when Bettina inquired as to the price of the pick of the litter. "Ten thousand dollars. But sorry, but the pick already has a commitment. All of Zenobia's picks are committed at least four years in advance. And there are three back-up commitments." Sybil squatted beside Zenobia. "In fact, the sonogram shows she'll be delivering eight pups. Seven of them are already spoken for. However, if you're so inclined, you can purchase the runt."

Bettina raised her head high. "I don't think you understand. This is for *Lily.*" She pointed to her daughter, who was hovering in a far corner.

The poor girl looked close to tears. "Mommy, it's okay. Maybe I don't need a puppy. Not one from a smelly, scary old dog, anyway."

Lily's *faux pas* were rare, but from the look on Sybil's face, this one would have to be addressed post haste if Bettina were to salvage the purchase. "What my daughter means to say is that she is humbled in the presence of Zenobia, and hopes she can live up to the honor of owning any one of the priceless pups blessed to be of her bloodline."

Sybil sighed. "I doubt she will. Perhaps a more suitable pet will be found at the SPCA? It's on Alabama Street." She reached for a pen and a notepad. In a moment she was scribbling what looked to be a street map. "From here, all you have to do is wind your way up Portola and back down the other side of the hill. Eventually, you'll hit Market. Then it's a short drive through the Mission to Alabama—"

Bettina snatched the pen from the woman's massive hand. She rummaged in her pocketbook until she found what she was looking for, her checkbook. Opening it, she turned back to Sybil. "I guess I'm not making myself clear. I'm willing to pay whatever it costs to ensure we get the pick of Zenobia's litter. How much did you say? Ten thousand?" She wrote out the check and signed it with a flourish.

"As I said before, that option is not on the table. More to the point, are you willing to take what I have to offer? Runts aren't show dogs, but they make great pets. You did say it was for your daughter, didn't you?"

"Yes, of course it's for Lily! But it's also for me! I mean, it will be our *family*'s dog."

"Good! Then we have an agreement." Sybil glared down at Bettina.

Bettina shrugged. Perhaps she was being silly. Who was to know if the dog were the pick or the runt? Besides, if she gave it enough vitamins, with its superior blood line, she had no doubt it could be another Caligula in no time.

"Okay then, I'll take the...*runt*." The word seemed to stick in her throat. "How much?"

Sybil snatched the check from her hand. "This will do."

Bettina grabbed it back again. "But ten thousand was for the pick!"

Sybil glared at her. "I never said that. You did. In fact, you said any dog with Zenobia's bloodline is 'priceless.' No arguments there. Take it or leave it. I have others who'll gladly pay the price."

Bettina glanced over at Zenobia. The dog had flopped down on her side beside her feed dish. Her wheezing was so loud that Lily had covered her ears with her hands.

Bettina couldn't blame her. The dog looked as if it would expire at any moment. And yet, she couldn't shake the memory of that massive stud Caligula. So grand! So noble! So obedient!

Slowly she let go of the check.

Sybil examined it before sticking it in her pocket. "Zenobia is due any day now. That said, her pups should be weaned by Valentine's Day."

"Here's hoping it's a happy birth day," Bettina muttered. "Come, Lily."

The little girl didn't have to be asked twice. She was out the door in a flash.

4:55 p.m.

USUALLY AT MIDDAY, TINY, GATED ALLYNE PARK, AT THE corner of Gough and Green, was filled with idlers playing hide-and-seek with any of the sun's rays that had found its way through the park's tallest redwoods. But at five o'clock on a blustery January evening, the sun had already dipped behind the grand old apartment building on the park's west side, leaving it empty except for a young collie and its owner, a father teaching his three-year-old son how to kick a soccer ball. The man's wife, large with child beneath her cashmere coat, sat on a nearby bench. She was reading the latest edition of the *Nob Hill Gazette*.

But no, they weren't alone. Brady was already there, sitting on one of the benches tucked behind a copse of Redwoods. When he saw Ally, he stood up. That's when she noticed he was holding two dozen long-stemmed roses: pale yellow, with tips that looked as if they'd been dipped in a warm pink paint.

She hesitated before opening the old wrought iron gate that separated her from the man she wished was free to love her.

Finally, she slid the gate's lock to one side. Each step she took toward him made it harder for her to stick to her decision to let him go.

"The florist called them 'Chicago Peace.'" He shrugged. "I just thought they were pretty."

She nodded. "They are. But really, Brady, you shouldn't have."

Realizing she wasn't going to take them, he dropped his

arm to his side. The stems were so long the petals almost touched the grass.

The collie came by and sniffed them, then crouched down, wagging his tail. When he realized Brady wasn't about to play with him, he leaped and pranced, then got back down on his haunches with a whine.

Brady laughed. "You see? He appreciates them. Why can't you?"

Ally shrugged. "I'm not the one you should be buying them for."

On the drive from Foot Fetish to the park, she had worked out everything she was going to say to him. Like how dropping Jade for her would ruin things for both Oliver and Zoe. And how Jade would be heartbroken.

Even if that didn't mean anything to Brady, it certainly mattered to Ally.

She was just about to launch into her argument for why they should keep it simple and just stay friends when she noticed something on his cheek: an eyelash.

She reached up very gently with her index and middle finger and whisked it away.

He took her fingers and placed them on his lips.

Slowly she pulled her fingers away. This left his lips hovering over hers.

She couldn't help herself. She kissed him.

No really, she devoured him.

When she felt his arms around her, she heard the collie barking like crazy, and she knew he had tossed the roses on the ground.

She also knew she wasn't going to be keeping her promise to herself, or to Jade.

She broke away, gasping for air. "I hate myself." She buried her head in her hands.

He tilted her head so that they were eye to eye again. "Why would you say that? Why do you feel that way?"

"Because…because I never wanted to be 'the other woman.'"

Brady shook his head in disbelief. "How can you be 'the other woman' if there is no first 'woman?'"

"Lower your voice, please." Ally nodded toward the family.

There was no way the mother could have overheard her. Still, almost as if she reading Ally mind, the woman slowly heaved herself off the bench and beckoned her husband to follow her out the gate. She whistled for the collie, too, but he leaped away before she could tether his collar to the leash in her hand. Seeing that the gate was already open, the dog scurried out. The woman chased behind him.

Realizing her dilemma, the woman's husband grabbed the soccer ball in one hand while he hoisted their son up onto his shoulders with the other, and headed out the gate after his wife.

One and a half kids and a dog, thought Ally. The typical American family. They love each other. They're building a life together. No clinging exes, no gay fake husbands. No need for a sperm donor in order to beat your biological clock…

No jumping through hoops to get into some silly club.

You choose what you lose in life, Ally conceded. *Brady will have to wait.*

"Brady, as much as you like to pretend otherwise, Jade is still in love with you. Yes, of course she wants to be a part of Oliver's life. But she also wants to be a part of yours."

He shook his head adamantly. "It's not going to happen. I've made that clear to her."

"Have you, really?" Ally cocked her head to one side. "Be honest. Since she's moved in, have the two of you... I'm asking you if you... Have you made love to her?"

His silence spoke volumes.

Finally, he turned his head toward the street. "Yes, you're right. I screwed up! And I wish things were different. But for the time being, they are what they are."

"That's why we can't move things forward. Not now, anyway." She dropped her head until she was staring at their entwined fingers. She marveled at his. They were long, lean and tan. She imagined them roaming all over her body, tempting her with his touch, opening her to his love...

The thought made her blush.

And it made her want him even more.

She opened her mouth to tell him so, to admit she couldn't live without him and that she was even willing to leave PHM&T if need be, when they heard the screech of tires and a bone-chilling scream.

Someone was shouting for an ambulance.

Instinctively both Brady and Ally's eyes went to the street corner. The family had left the gate open, and the collie, frantic, ran back into the park, barking and growling before it leaped back out again.

By the time Ally and Brady reached the street, a crowd had gathered. One man was routing cars around the father, who lay in the street, screaming in pain. His legs and arms were askew like a broken doll. The leash was in his hand. The driver of the car that must have hit him was leaning over him, chanting his apology like a desperate mantra, over and over again.

The stricken man's wife struggled to hold her wailing son in her arms before the boy ran into the street to comfort his father. She shifted her gaze toward the park. Seeing Ally, she screamed, "Look at what you've done! Looked what you've done!"

Is she right? Ally wondered. *Did I leave the gate open when I entered the park? No, I couldn't have…*

Oh my God! What have I done?

But no, the woman wasn't screaming at Ally. She was shouting at the collie.

The dog whined mournfully before trotting off down the street, morose and lost.

Ashamed, Ally turned around. Her instinct was to go back into the park. But why? It wasn't as if she could turn back the clock.

There was nothing waiting for her there.

As she sobbed, Brady cradled her head to his chest.

She stayed there in his arms until the ambulance came and left with the injured man and his family. Slowly, the crowd dissolved, and cars once again glided right over the spot where the man had lain.

"I should drive you home," Brady murmured in her ear.

"No!" She shook her head. "No. You should leave."

As if reading her mind, he said, "It's not your fault, Ally. I know for a fact you closed the gate. And even if you had left it open, the accident could have been caused by any number of variables. The driver of the car should've been more alert. Or maybe he shouldn't have been going so fast. At the very least, the damn dog should have been on a leash!"

"I don't want the guilt, Brady! It hurts too much!"

"You're overreacting. You're projecting your feelings about...about us onto this freak accident."

Before he could say another word, she put her fingers on his lips. She remembered doing that before. It seemed like a million years ago.

"Let's go home and hold our babies," she whispered. "I'll call you, soon."

She allowed him to walk her to her car.

They both knew the decision she had already made.

Still, she knew he'd wait for her call.

CHAPTER FIVE

Thursday, 10 January
1:48 p.m.

"Who was that on the phone?" asked Lorna.

She'd been pacing impatiently by the front door for the past twenty minutes in anticipation of her mother's arrival. "Was it Hera? She rarely comes into the city. And when she does, she gets lost at the drop of a hat. If need be, I can meet her down at the corner of Van Ness and Vallejo, to show her how to get up here—"

"Whoa! Calm down and take a deep breath." Matthew's soft, soothing tone was the same one he used when he played with Dante. "It was only Bettina. She wanted you to meet her at Mother's today to go over the details of the Easter egg hunt. I told her you had to hang here."

"Oh my God! You didn't tell her why, did you?" The

thought of Bettina barging in on them in order to meet Hera, only to diss her to anyone within hearing distance— particularly Eleanor—was too much for Lorna to bear.

He laughed. "Hey, I'm no fool. I told her Dante had a play date. I figure she wouldn't show her face here if she thought a battalion of one-year-olds were underfoot."

The tension went out of Lorna's shoulders. "That was smart thinking on your part. And it is a 'play date' of sorts."

The crunch of car wheels on the driveway brought the trepidation back to her face. She ran to the window. Yes, it was her mother. She had come in a brand new Leaf. That was to be expected.

But Hera wasn't alone. A pale bald man with a hawk nose, wearing almost sheer, white flowing robes, got out of the car, too.

"Battle stations," Lorna murmured under her breath as Matthew opened the front door.

৯৯

"YOUR AURA IS NICE, MATTHEW." HERA TILTED HER HEAD AS she examined her son-in-law. "A bright pink. The telltale sign of a tender and passionate soul. What a wonderful counterbalance to Lorna's! She's been a cloudy blue for so many years now."

At a loss for how to answer, Matthew gave a thumbs-up to his mother-in-law.

Lorna stifled a groan. She was a cloudy blue, eh? She'd been around Hera's mumbo jumbo all her life. She knew that in ReikiSpeak Hera had just pegged her as being fearful of the future and indecisive.

Scared.

She may have been right once, but not now, Lorna thought. The cost of fear is too high. It's Dante's wellbeing.

Lorna glowered at her mother. "I thought I made it clear that you were to come alone."

Hera's smile faltered, but only for a moment. "You specifically said I couldn't bring the shaman, so I didn't." She raised a thin arm in the direction of her companion. "You know very well that a swami is someone very different." Before Lorna could contradict her, Hera held out her arms to Matt. "Ah, and our little man here. May I hold him? So pale and yellow is his glow! Swami B, you see it too, don't you?"

The man in the flowing robes bobbed his head. "Yes, Hera, this child is an old soul! A healer in his own right."

"One day, maybe." Hera clapped her hands together. "Wouldn't that be wonderful?"

"Mother, I told you about Dante's condition. He'll have his own issues to work through."

"Yes, dear Lorna. That is what Swami B and I are here for." She nodded at the man.

"Swami B?" Matt asked. "The B stands for…what? Bailey? Brown? Berkowitz?"

The swami shrugged. "Brownstein."

Matt squinted at him. "I thought you looked familiar! Aren't you the guy on that infomercial about those tricked-out timeshares?"

"Good eye! Used to be. Then the Great Recession brought me enlightenment."

Hera snapped her fingers in front of his face. "Enough already. I paid you to do a healing, remember? It's time to commence."

Swami B put his hands on Dante's head and muttered a fast and furious chant, but the little boy obviously didn't like it because he moaned and squirmed.

Lorna slapped the man's hands away. "Stop it! You're scaring him!"

"Lorna! How dare you?" Hera's voice trembled. "We came all this way, and this is how you treat us?"

"I asked you here because I thought you cared about me and wanted to be involved in my life." Lorna's tears felt like hot coals on her cheeks. "All I'm asking is that you be sensitive to my son's needs and respect our wishes for him. Mother—*Hera*—really! Is that too much to ask?"

The clouds of anger faded in Hera's eyes. She nodded. But before she could speak, the doorbell chimed.

Frustration fell heavy on Lorna's lids. She took a deep breath, opened her eyes, and then headed for the front door.

Bettina stood in front of her.

"I came for a hug from my little nephew," Bettina purred. "Where is the little prince?"

Lorna couldn't believe her ears. "Really? Now? Like, right this very moment?" Without thinking, she glanced toward the living room, where Hera held court.

Noting the direction of Lorna's concerned glance, Bettina

plucked Dante from her sister-in-law's arms and swept past her.

Aw hell, thought Lorna.

She steeled herself for the worst and said a little prayer.

❦

"REALLY? YOU'RE LORNA'S MOTHER?" BETTINA LOOKED FROM Hera to Lorna and back again. But as best as she could, she averted her eyes from the bald man who wore nothing under his sheer robe. The way his *thing* hung there, dangling free and easy, was utterly disgusting. Who was this guy, anyway?

Well, if anything, her mother raised her with manners. She turned to the man, but kept her eyes pinned on his eyes. "And you're Lorna's father, I take it?"

Hera's brow almost hit the crown of her silvery buzz cut. "You're too presumptuous, dear. I've come with a friend. Sadly, Lorna's father and I parted ways many years ago. Before she was born, in fact."

Bettina smiled. "Ah! I see!" She'd figured as much. Not only was Lorna's mother some old hippy, as it turns out, she'd had Lorna out of wedlock, too.

Bettina was beside herself. *Wait until Mother hears this,* she thought. Thank goodness she'd rushed over when she did.

It had pissed her off royally when Matt told her that Lorna was "too busy" to drop what she was doing in order to meet her and go over the Easter egg hunt details. Then, when Matt let it slip that Dante was in the middle of a play date, naturally she'd jumped to the conclusion that it was with Jade and Oliver, so she hurried right over. Brady's investment in Matt's startup scheme could limit his financial liquidity and ruin Art's chance to talk to him regarding other investment opportunities.

Bettina couldn't let that happen.

As far as she was concerned, Art's redemption would take more than an apology. Even a vow of celibacy wouldn't do it. Not that he was capable of either. Once a sick pervert, always a sick pervert.

Art's only chance of staying in her good graces was to secure Brady Pierce's investment portfolio for his financial firm. Their double date with the Pierces was the first step in accomplishing that. It was the only hope she had of recouping her own losses with her husband.

The financial ones, anyway.

The emotional ones would always stand between them.

Bettina looked over at Matt. The concern in his eyes for Lorna made her want to laugh and cry at the same time. Her brother was such a fool. She gave Dante a squeeze. Well, at least he had a beautiful son to console him.

And now, she'd been presented the perfect opportunity in which to embarrass Lorna in front of Eleanor. "Hera, welcome to the family! In fact, I'm sure my mother, Eleanor, would love to meet you, too! I think a family dinner is called for!"

Hera smiled. "I look forward to it. However, I won't be available until May."

Bettina sighed her disappointment. "A shame. Leaving the country?" She wouldn't have been surprised in the least to learn that Hera was on the lam. She'd take a quick perusal of Interpol's Watch List when she got home. Finding Lorna's mother there would be icing on the cake.

Hera's laughter was as light as a wind chime. "No, I'm staying put. But my calling is to guide new souls safely through the birth canal! New friendships, new relationships, new beginnings…"

And a new way to torture Lorna, Bettina thought. *Lorna's mother is some sort of New Age doula? How perfectly grotesque!* "We'll make it May, then. In fact, how about Mother's Day? I'm sure you—and Matt and my mother, Eleanor—will agree that it's the perfect day to bring all our families together!"

Hera nodded. "Then Mother's Day it is!"

Bettina smiled. The look of horror on Lorna's face was priceless.

❧

LORNA WAS RELIEVED THAT MATT TOOK THE INITIATIVE TO WALK Bettina out. She was too numb to do so herself.

Her only wish was that Bettina would never darken her doorstep again.

She turned to her mother. "Bettina can be pushy. Listen, if you're too busy on Mother's Day, I can always make up some sort of excuse to get you out of it."

"On the contrary! I wouldn't miss it for the world." Hera shrugged. "No wonder you've stayed away all these years.

You've done well with Matt, but that sister of his! Talk about bad karma."

Lorna's heart leaped in her chest. "Then, you like Matt?"

"Of course I do. What's not to like? He's a handsome man. He worships you, and"—Hera looked around at Lorna's well-appointed living room—"you want for nothing."

Nothing except a happy and healthy son, Lorna thought. "Hera, Bettina doesn't know about Dante's condition."

Her mother snorted. "I'm not surprised! That Bettina woman is blind to her own emotions, so no doubt she can't read them in others."

"Matt and I would prefer to tell her—and Eleanor, for that matter—when we feel the time is right."

Hera shrugged. "You can't hold back the truth, Lorna. It has its own free will. Don't be afraid of where it might take you."

She kissed her daughter. Then she nudged Swami B out of his trance and led him to the front door.

3: 14 p.m.

"YOU WOULD HAVE BEEN SHOCKED, MOTHER! IT WAS AN absolute freak show! I thought I was in the Haight or something! In fact, I think I smelled pot on the pair of them." Bettina shivered for effect. "Her head was practically shaved. Not to mention it's half gray! I'm not talking highlights,

Mother. Just...*gray*. Bland. Blah. I don't think this woman—Hera is her name, believe it or not, like some Egyptian goddess or something!—I don't think she's ever seen the inside of a hair salon! The woman needs a serious makeover."

"Greek," Eleanor murmured. She didn't look up, but stayed with the chore at hand: icing a cake.

Bettina looked up sharply. "What's that supposed to mean?"

"It means you've got it wrong. The goddess, Hera? She's Greek." Eleanor sighed. "And Lorna's mother doesn't live in the Haight. She's from Bolinas. Has been there for years. In fact, she's a pillar of the community...if you can call it that. Actually, it's more like a commune. Do people still use that word, 'commune?'"

Bettina stared at her mother. "How would I know? And why is it that you know so much about this...this person?"

"Because I had her investigated years ago." Eleanor stopped to face her daughter. "When it was obvious to me that Matt was smitten with Lorna and nothing I said could change his opinion, I felt it my duty to run a background check."

Bettina nodded. "A necessary evil. Perfectly understandable."

"Maybe. But finding out why Lorna was so evasive about her family didn't really change anything, now did it? He loved her then and loves her more even now. It also made me realize why Lorna was so driven academically. With two deadbeat hippies for parents, she felt she had something to prove." Eleanor shook her head in awe. "Well, I guess she proved it. To me, anyway."

Bettina couldn't believe her ears. She'd come here to crow, but once again, Eleanor had taken Lorna's side.

"You're too kind, Mother. You're always giving Lorna the benefit of the doubt. I wish I could do the same, but she has no loyalty to our family. She has no loyalty *to me!*" Bettina spit out the words.

"Dear, what in hell are you talking about?"

If Bettina was going to bury Lorna once and for all, the place and time was here and now. "Your sweet, darling Lorna found out that Art…that Art was cheating on me, and she kept quiet about it!"

"Ah. I see." Eleanor thought for a while. Finally, she said, "I wouldn't have told you either."

"What? How can you say that?"

Eleanor took her daughter's hand. "Bettina, let me ask you a question. Would you have told Lorna if you knew Matthew had taken a lover?"

Touché. Of course they both know she wouldn't—and not out of loyalty to Matthew, but because Bettina would enjoy knowing and keeping it a secret.

Eleanor placed her hand on Bettina's cheek. "You always put your father on a pedestal, but what you didn't know is that your father has had numerous affairs."

"Father?" Bettina couldn't believe her ears.

"Sadly, yes. My friends knew. They also knew better than to hurt me with the knowledge. Why tell me? It's not as if I would have ever left him. If anything, I would have hated them, not him."

But that's just it, Mother, Bettina thought. *I would want to be the messenger. I would want her to hate me.*

"Bettina, darling, if you're having troubles in your marriage, the solution is simple. Spend less time with that damn club of yours, and more time with your husband."

That was it for Bettina. She stormed out the door.

She didn't start her car immediately, but sat in Eleanor's driveway. It was just a mile between her home and Eleanor's, but she was too shaken up to trust herself behind the wheel.

She knew her mother was right. The more distant she felt from Art, the more important the club seemed to her.

And yet, Bettina still refused to talk to Art about anything, let alone his affair and his fetish.

Since his New Year's Eve indiscretion, every time Art walked into a room, she walked out of it. She still couldn't face him. He must finally have noticed because lately he'd call after her, sometimes chasing her down the hall. Even in heels she ran faster, and she was sure to lock the door after her. But he refused to take the hint. Instead, he'd stand outside the door, pleading for her attention, claiming he'd been "a very bad boy."

At such times, she was too mortified to even consider what he wanted from her.

Maybe he wanted her to…

Oh. My. God.

Well! If that's the case, he can beg all he wants, because I can't! *I won't.*

He'd enjoy it too much.

3:44 p.m.

KIMBERLEY SAVITCH HAD AN AXE TO GRIND. PREFERABLY ON THE back of Jade Pierce's pretty little neck.

She was more determined than ever to get Brady's wife ousted from the club. It would be just payback for his jilting her, once his wife's membership was formalized.

To get herself out of her funk, she treated herself to a spa day. About damn time, too. The last one she'd had, she'd treated herself to a vajazzle, in the shape of a Christmas bell to celebrate the holidays.

Alas, it had been a waste of money. Her husband was always too tired after work for sex, and Brady had quit calling.

While an esthetician toiled downtown with hot wax and a paintbrush, Kimberley ruminated on her next course of action.

Her mission: get Brady back.

Or get the revenge she sought for his dumping her.

She'd hoped that by now Jade had found the purple thong she'd left in the Pierce's kitchen cabinet on Thanksgiving morning. But there hadn't been any teary repercussions, let alone a break-up.

"Hell," Kimberley growled under her breath, "I'll bet she

never opened the cabinet because she never cooked a meal in her life!"

She was certain Lily's disappearance and subsequent panic in the corn maze would cost Jade her membership in the Onesies. How maddening it was to hear Bettina—Lily's own mother—come to Jade's defense!

Just as the esthetician applied the final hot wax strip to Kimberley's mound, a solution presented itself. *Jade's naivety is the key to getting Brady back.*

Just as the old saying suggested: keep your friends close, and your enemies closer. *I'll snuggle up to Jade. She's so insecure that in no time at all, we'll be BFFs. Better yet, I'll promise her my vote for the Onesies Top Mom!*

Kimberley was so excited she sat straight up. The esthetician, taken off guard, yanked a few more hairs than needed.

Kimberley squealed like a banshee.

"Oh my god! I'm so *sorry!*" the woman screamed back at her.

Kimberley was afraid to look down. But from the look on the woman's face, her guess was that major damage control would be needed.

"Um… how would you feel about a moustache instead of a heart?" the esthetician asked meekly. "They're coming back in vogue, you know."

"How would you feel about forgoing your tip?" Kimberley countered. "Oh, hell, just take it all off! In fact, let's add a few stones: Can you spell out 'Brady?'"

Relieved, the woman nodded and got back to work.

Kimberley knew that the odds her husband would be up

for sex were slim to none. He'd never notice. Hell, he'd never even *see* it.

It was time to get Brady back, and fast.

She remembered Jade's trepidation at her Top Moms challenge task, coordinating an advanced placement course for the Fivesies. She'd call Jade first thing in the morning and offer to give her a few suggestions over a coffee date after their PHM&T group meet-ups.

Brady would be hers again in no time. Certainly before the stones fell out of her vajazzle.

CHAPTER SIX

Friday, 11 January

"You never called." Brady tried to sound nonchalant, but he knew he wasn't succeeding.

He caught Ally just as she was leaving the Marina library's children's story hour. He overheard Jade talking on the phone to one of the other PHM&T mothers who was trying to set up a coffee date, informing her that perhaps they could rendezvous at the Moscone Park's playground afterward, which was adjacent to the library.

Perfect, he thought.

He'd make sure to take his jog around the neighborhood right at that time. That way, he could pass the library just as she was coming out. Unlike Ally, who was always out the door after the meet-ups with her list of errands firmly in hand, Jade dawdled afterward, sometimes gossiping with the other moms, sometimes searching frantically for where she left Oliver's jacket or his tiny mittens and hat.

If Brady were lucky, he'd find Ally's car parked on one of the side streets and he could intercept her there, away from prying eyes. Unfortunately, her car was parked right in front of the library. *Damn,* he thought. Still, he had to chance it.

True to form, Ally was the first of the Onesies moms out the door. She stopped short when she saw him leaning up against her car, then she practically ran to him.

In another time, place or universe, she'd be jumping into his arms. But he knew the here and now made that impossible.

And whatever she said to him, now that they were face to face, might mean he'd never feel the joy of her lips pressed against his ever again.

He had to know, one way or another. It was why he had sought her out.

"Showing up here was not one of your brightest ideas, Brady," Ally muttered, as she unbuckled Zoe from her stroller. Seeing him, Zoe cooed and bounced, making it difficult for Ally to hold onto her while she scrounged for her keys in the baby bag perched on her shoulder.

"Here, let me help." He reached for Zoe, who practically leaped into his arms. Surprised but pleased, he turned red and tried to laugh it off.

He wished Ally would laugh with him.

She wasn't even smiling. "You're right. I should have called you before now. I owe you that. Please forgive me."

"I'm not here to make you feel guilty." He kept a smile on

his face, despite the fact that his heart was being ripped from his chest. "I'm also not here to pressure you in any way."

"I know you wouldn't do that, Brady." She reached out to touch his arm, but stopped short. Glancing at the library's floor-to-ceiling windows, she murmured, "That terrible car accident the other day rattled me. It's incredible the way our lives can turn on a dime."

Seeing he was about to protest, she added, "Yes, I know. But taking risks or a leap of faith, can pay off, too. Believe me, Brady, my whole life is a perfect example of that. It's why I broke off and started my own company. It's also why I had Zoe on my own. And it's why I took the risk of selling my company to a conglomerate that I feel can expand it, with or without me. Each decision was a risk. But it was also the best move I could make at the time." Sadness glistened in her eyes. "I love you, and I believe you when you say you love me too. But the timing is off for the risk you present. We both know that. We have our children to consider."

He nodded. The lump in his throat made it too hard for him to speak.

"Good. Thank you for understanding, and for not making this any harder than it already is." Her eyes shifted toward the library. "And just in time. Jade just walked out. She sees us, and she's headed this way. By the way, Bracknell industries would like you to sit on the board. If she asks, you can say it's what we talked about. And if you want to accept, the next meeting is on the Tuesday, February fifth at six o'clock. We do dinner in the corporate dining room—"

"What….Bracknell? Wow!" He shook his head confused.

One minute she's breaking up with me, the next, she's presenting me with a prestigious corporate board seat.

My consolation prize, I guess.

"Yeah sure, count me in." If only because it presented him with a legitimate reason to see her.

He mimicked Ally's bland grin as he waved at Jade. But his smile wavered when he saw who was walking over with her—Kimberley Savitch.

Jade is hanging with Madame Ovary? When the hell did that happen?

"In fact, let me fill her in on it," Ally murmured under her breath. "That way, she won't feel threatened. Of course, Kimberley can't know about it. Do you think you can keep her busy for a few minutes?"

He tried to keep the smile on his face. "I'm sure I can find something to say to her."

❧

"WHAT'S WRONG, LOVER BOY? AREN'T YOU HAPPY TO SEE ME?" The way Kimberley tenderly rocked her two-year-old son who was resting happily in her arms, you'd think she was Mother Teresa.

Brady knew better.

"What the hell do you think you're doing?" He tried to keep his voice jovial so that he didn't scare her little brat, or Oliver for that matter.

"Just making a new friend. I presume you have no objection."

"In fact, I do." He leaned in and hissed, "Stay away from me, and stay away from my family."

"If I do, I'll have to explain to Jade why I can't come out and play. Frankly, I don't think she'll like the answer."

"Whatever you say to Jade won't matter. She knows I've…that I've slipped up on occasion."

"Oh? So you two have some sort of 'understanding?' Well, that should make things easier for us, wouldn't you say?" She winked at him. "In fact, if you want to soften the blow, invite her to join us, if you like. I've never tried a threesome, but Jade strikes me as the adventurous type."

The anger in his eyes must have scared her because Kimberley suddenly teared up. "Don't you get it, Brady? I'd do anything to be with you. I'll even—I'll even hang with your skanky wife."

Had she not called Jade a skank, he might have actually felt sorry for her.

Instead, he wanted to bury her alive.

The best way to do so was to call her bluff. "Hey, Jade," he called out. "When you've got a moment, Kimberley has a question for you."

Without even turning to her, he murmured, "Go for it, Kimberley. Tell her about us. See what she does with the information. Oh, by the way, tomorrow night, we're having dinner with Bettina Cross. What do you think Jade will say to her about it? My bet is that it's a tastier tidbit than anything they'll have on the menu."

Jade waved back. She wasn't smiling. Still, he felt some

relief when Jade crossed her heart and shook Ally's hand before coming over to them.

The blood drained from Kimberley's face. But by the time Jade was at their side, her color had returned, and she was all smiles again.

"What's up?" Jade asked as she gave Brady a knowing wink, and entwined her arm in his.

"I was wondering…" Kimberley glanced up at Brady.

What she saw was a face he'd perfected in a million boardroom confrontations: *perfect calm.*

"I was wondering if instead of coffee, how about we have lunch together? We have so much to go over." Kimberley's voice shook just enough for Brady to know he had won this round.

Jade looked up at Brady. "Honey, do you mind? It's club business. You know how badly I want to win this Top Mom thingy!"

"Not at all," Brady said cheerfully. "In fact, while you girls grab a bite, why don't I look after these two bruisers, right here in the park?" He ruffled the tufts on top of their sons' heads. "And lunch is on me, okay?"

It was a small price to pay for Kimberley's silence.

CHAPTER SEVEN

Saturday, 18 January

FOR THE SAKE OF HIS SANITY, BRADY HOPED THE MEN'S ROOM AT Ozumo had only one head, and a lock on the door, too.

No such luck. When he excused himself, Art jumped up, too.

Art shrugged as he fell into step with Brady. "Lots of premium sake and a tiny bladder is a bad combo."

So are you and my money, Brady thought.

The sooner he could let Art know he had no intention of investing with him, the better.

Even before the dinner, he'd done his homework on Art Cross, and the reconnaissance coming back was not good. If Art was able to wangle a savvy investor or two, they left him pretty quickly once they realized he didn't know his ass from his elbow when it came to picking winners and losers.

If he wasn't suffering from hold-a-phobia, he was shorting all the wrong stocks.

"He uses so many different credit lines, he would make Madoff dizzy," one of Brady's sources whispered. "In fact, word has it that he's practically bankrupted his wife's estate."

No way, no how was Brady going to let Art anywhere near *his* portfolio.

Throughout the meal, Brady kept the topic on sports, segueing from the Warriors' offensive game to the 49ers' luck at securing a top playoff seed with home-field advantage. If there was a lull in the conversation, he plugged it with a question about Lily's ballet aspirations. After that, he could count on Bettina's pride to fill the gap.

Frankly, he was somewhat annoyed that Jade had hardly said a word. On the way over, he had filled her in on Art's reputation and asked her to do her bit to steer the conversation to safer topics.

"This dinner date was your idea," he reminded her. "I realize it's to Oliver's benefit that we stay on their good side, but I'll be damned if I'm going to piss away my hard-earned money with Bettina's deadbeat husband. You'll have to come up with a better way to impress her."

Now he knew why his ex-wife had held her tongue, metaphorically speaking.

Art waited until he was midstream, then started his hard sell. "So listen, Brady, I know for the little ladies' sakes we've been perfect gentleman and kept the subject of investing off the table, but I've got a couple of market plays that I think will be right up your alley."

Brady shook his head. "Save it, Art. I have one hard and fast rule—I don't invest with friends."

Art frowned. "Oh no? What about your investment in Matt's start-up?"

Brady shrugged. He had him there. "When he approached me about it, it was merely a business proposition. His business plan is solid, and it had nothing to do with how close our wives have become in the meantime."

"Seriously? Quit pulling my pudd. Oops, sorry! Poor choice of words, considering where we're standing—" Art's smile curdled into a vicious snarl. "And considering your wife's former profession."

Brady's stare was cold. "What the hell is that supposed to mean?"

"Didn't Jade tell you? She and I go way back. Don't tell me you thought your pole was the only one she was rubbing up against in that back room at the Condor Club. Look at it this way. You won't just be investing with a friend, but a friend *with benefits*."

That was it for Brady. He turned toward Art and aimed for his crotch.

Bull's-eye.

"What the hell?" Art leaped back, but it was too late. He was soaked.

He was still sputtering as Brady zipped up and went to the sink to wash his hands.

But as Brady headed for the door, Art yelled out after him, "You know, Bettina isn't wise to Jade's past. Not yet, anyway. I'm guessing it'll make great dinner conversation. Not just tonight, but later this week, with all the ladies in the club."

Brady stopped. He didn't turn around when he muttered, "A million. No more. And I want a verified prospectus of the past week's earnings sent by courier every Monday." He turned his head just far enough to catch Art's eye in the mirror. "If I hear that you've spoken to Jade—if you dare to even look at her—the deal is off."

Art shrugged. "Sure, whatever. She's not my type anyway."

Art yelped as Brady rammed him up against the wall. But Brady's fist stopped just short of Art's nose.

Brady left Art with his knee propped up on the sink, drying his pants with the restroom hand dryer.

Back at the table, both men were smart enough to keep up the sports banter, and to smile and laugh when their wives said anything clever.

Brady picked up the tab on the dinner, which ran just under a thousand dollars. The only reason he left a generous tip was because their server was his favorite, Anna, and he wasn't about to take out his anger at Art and Jade on her.

He knew his silence on the drive home was making Jade anxious, but he couldn't care less. She finally got up the nerve to ask, "How…how did you think it went?"

"I gave him a million to play with, and that's the end of it."

She exhaled and smiled.

"All this means is your past with the Condor Club is safe. For now, anyway. And as long as Bettina doesn't get wind of it and kick you out, you can keep taking Oliver to the meet-ups, and you can hang with your friends all you want." He looked over at her, catching her face in the passing street-lights as her smile faded with every word he spoke. "But as far as you and I are concerned, we're no more than two people sharing a house and a child. I no longer want you in my bed, Jade. If this arrangement doesn't work for you, you're free to leave—no harm, no foul."

When they pulled into the garage, he didn't walk over to her side of the car and open her door. Instead, he walked up the steps and into the house.

He didn't know when or if she finally left the car for one of the home's many guest rooms because it was long after he paid the sitter and had gone to bed.

At least he couldn't hear her crying three stories below.

CHAPTER EIGHT

Monday, 4 February

"Okay now, be honest with me, Caleb. Which is your favorite? It's the cranberry pear, isn't it? You gobbled it up the quickest, so that has to be it."

Jillian pointed to the pie farthest to the right side of her kitchen counter, a necessary maneuver since both Addison and Amelia were into climbing on furniture *and* into pie. During Caleb Martin's taste test, she'd made sure they were occupied on the kitchen rug with her plastic cookie cutters and a few errant mixing bowls. Their TwinSpeak was more than gibberish now. Real words were lining up into real sentences. Jillian was so proud of them.

Still, her favorite baby phrase was "ah-poo pie."

Caleb chewed and swallowed quickly, but before he could answer her, she nudged another pie forward. "Hold on! If I remember correctly, you had two big wedges of the coconut chocolate walnut."

He nodded, then held up a cautionary finger as he gulped down his coffee.

That didn't stop her from declaring, "But wait! No fair answering until you try this one, too!" Her eyes opened wide as she grabbed a pie from the far corner of the counter and nudged it his way. "It's called an 'Apple Jack.' It's got Granny Smiths drenched in Jack Daniels, topped with a sea salt caramel sauce."

He groaned, but stuck his fork in it anyway.

Jillian pursed her lips in anticipation of his answer.

She had to wait until he was satisfied with four more forkfuls. Finally, he moaned blissfully and patted his stomach. "Jillian, doll, you're killing me here! I'll be the fattest forest ranger in the Presidio."

She plopped down on his lap and nuzzled his neck. "You're such a tease! Just look at these six-pack abs." In a blink of an eye, her fingers unbuttoned his shirt. She stopped to admire his hairy chest. "Don't ever take off your shirt in the woods, or every female hiker will go crazy."

"Trust me, they'd run in the opposite direction. They'll think I'm a grizzly." He laughed. "Or worse! Sasquatch!"

Jillian shrugged. "Scott was as hairless as a Chihuahua. I guess he spent his lunches getting manscaped."

Caleb grinned. "You make him sound like such a pussy."

His remark stopped her cold. Her smile faded.

Seeing it disappear, his did, too. "You're also still in love with him, aren't you?"

Jillian pretended she didn't hear him. "What do you think—was the crust on the Apple Jack flaky enough? If it wasn't—"

"I thought so." Caleb shoved his plate away. "Guess it's time to waddle off into the sunset."

"No! Wait!" She reached for his arm. "Caleb, we were married for ten years. We had two children together. I thought I'd be spending the rest of my life with him. And now…"

"And now you're not." He shrugged. "He's got some other woman in his life. And you've got me, remember?"

She nodded. "Yes. He's got her, and I…I have you." The first tear fell before she could turn her head, or wipe it away.

He stepped back from her. "And I'm the one who loves you. I have since the moment I saw you running down the street, screaming after the girls' runaway stroller."

She almost choked as her sobs turned to giggles, but just for a moment as he continued, "But Jillian, *I'm not him*. And I'll never be anything like him, either. Considering how he treats you, don't you think that's a good thing?"

She should have screamed "Yes" at the top of her lungs.

She wanted to, really she did, but there was still too much of Scott there in the house. In her memories.

As if reading her mind, Caleb picked up his coat and walked out the front door.

She started to run after him, to call him back, but the crash behind her stopped her dead in her tracks.

One of the girls had yanked the tablecloth. The pies and plates had fallen to the floor. Both girls now sported pie-tin hats. Whatever filling and crust they weren't wearing was making its way into their mouths as they scooped up the goodies with their plump little fingers.

Jillian plopped down on the floor to cry. Instead, she laughed.

CHAPTER NINE

Tuesday, 5 February

"Well, well, well," Ellis muttered to Ally. "Your Mr. Pierce handled himself admirably. He's been a big hit with Mr. Bracknell."

Ally turned toward the conference room's window, where Brady stood with Laurence Bracknell, admiring the incomparable bay and city views afforded them from the highest floor in the renowned Transamerica Pyramid Center.

During the meeting, she too had been impressed. It was a side of Brady she'd never seen before. After she'd given him a formal introduction, Brady turned on the charm. He was modest about his accomplishments, thoughtful in the questions he asked, and tactful in the answers he gave when asked to comment on the issues facing the board.

Brady earned me big brownie points, Ally thought. *Just in time, too, considering it's been almost a month since I gave Ellis my proposal.* "By the way, Ellis, how did Mr. Bracknell respond to my prospectus on the pie shop?"

Ellis hesitated, then shrugged. "Sorry, old girl. You'll get an answer by May. By then we'll have better cash flow and we may be looking for something different to do with it."

She tried not to show her disappointment.

"How did the two of you meet again?" Ellis sounded innocent enough, but she knew him too well. Every question was a probe. Every declaration had an ulterior motive. Everyone was his stepping-stone to Mr. Bracknell's side.

Just then, Brady looked over at her and waved.

Ellis raised a brow.

Ignoring it, Ally smiled innocently. "His son is in my daughter's playgroup. He sold AStealAtThisPrice.com in order to be a stay-at-home father."

"How noble." Ellis shrugged. "I'm sure he finds hanging in the park with all you yummy mommies an added benefit."

Before Ally could retort, Mr. Bracknell beckoned her over.

Ally waved back, then murmured, "You're behind the times, Ellis. All the best business contacts are made on the playground. You should go sometime with your family. Oh sorry, I forgot you're not married! Too bad because just hanging out might seem a bit pervy." She paused, as if a thought just came to her. "Hey, there's an idea for you. Why not just rent a kid?'"

From the look on his face, she could tell he was actually thinking that through.

❧

"A**H**, **HERE'S OUR LITTLE STAR NOW!**" T**HE WAY** L**AURENCE** Bracknell put his arm around Ally's shoulders and squeezed her, you would have thought she was his long lost daughter. "Your ears must be burning from all the praise."

Ally blushed. "It's always great to be appreciated."

"You've done the corporation a great service, convincing Brady to join us."

Brady laughed. "It didn't take much arm-twisting. Your portfolio speaks for itself."

"You and Ally know better than anyone—consumers are a fickle bunch. Capturing their attention and keeping it isn't easy. The knowledge you bring to the board is invaluable."

"You've got a great head start with Ms. Thornton. Where she leads, I follow. She's a genius at sniffing out trends."

Better make hay while the sun is shining, Ally thought. She smiled brightly. "My pie shop concept is a great example. It's going to be the next big dessert craze."

Laurence's face went blank. "Really? A pie shop? What a unique concept. Too bad I hadn't heard of it before now." He leaned in conspiratorially. "On the QT, just this morning Bracknell purchased Toppers, the cupcake chain. It was Ellis's lead."

Ellis? Ally fumed. *Why that lying son of a bitch! Laurence never even saw my proposal!*

"The due diligence shows he's was right about it. Very successful, and lots of growth on the horizon," Laurence continued. "That young man keeps his ear to the ground! He was the one who brought Foot Fetish to our attention." Noting her dismay, Laurence patted her shoulder. "That's not to say your pie idea isn't a good one. But catching a wave means doing more than dipping your toe in the water every now and then. You've got to get in the deep end and swim with the rest of us sharks. Whenever you're ready to come back full time, you let me know."

§

"DID YOU HEAR WHAT HE SAID?" ALLY'S THIRD MARTINI MADE her both morose and tipsy. "Titan of industry Laurence Bracknell called me a *guppy*! Me, whose company produced nineteen percent of his total net income in the third quarter!" To make her point, she thrust her martini glass at Brady's chest.

The old me would be putting the move on her, now that her defenses are down, Brady thought. *But the new me will be a perfect gentleman...*

His resolve melted away when the spaghetti strap of her dress fell off her shoulder.

He held tight to his scotch tumbler, willing himself to resist the urge to move the flimsy piece of silk back where it belonged.

Worse yet, he wanted to strip her down altogether.

He sighed. "You've got it all wrong. His exact phrase was

that he welcomed you to swim with him and the rest of the sharks."

"I did. I mean, I am! I gave the sniveling brown-noser, Ellis, a full prospectus on the pie shop business I want to take national. And I asked him to show Bracknell, so that I might get the initial funding. Do you know what he did with it? Buried it! Apparently at the bottom of the sea where he and the other sharks are circling each other."

She waved down the bartender for another martini.

"A pie shop? That sounds hot."

Ally toasted Brady with her empty glass. "That's what I thought, too! And with Jillian's pies, the lines will be out the door."

"You've got that right. She's one hell of a baker. Do you think she's up for it?"

"You betcha. Rarin' to go, in fact. She needs the cash flow, what with that horrid divorce and all. But now I have to tell her it's going to take longer than we thought."

Brady shrugged. "It doesn't have to. Why don't you send the prospectus my way? Maybe it's something I'd like to invest in."

"Really? Wow, Brady, thanks!" Without thinking, Ally threw her arms around his neck.

He knew he shouldn't do it, but his lips brushed her forehead. Her hair smelled like roses, just as he remembered from the other night.

Maybe it was because he surprised her. Or maybe she was too tipsy to know what she was doing. Whatever the reason, she looked up at him and said, "I love you, too."

He had to kiss her.

She didn't resist. At least, not at first.

Then she jerked herself away. "I'm...so sorry. I didn't mean to... We promised each other..." She buried her head in her hands.

He knew why. She was trying to hide her tears.

Finally, she pulled her hands away. But she wouldn't look up at him. "When I told Jade about this opportunity to sit on the Bracknell board, I also made it clear that if she did not want you to do so, the offer would be withdrawn. Just so you know, she told me she hated the thought of you having this excuse to spend time with me, but at the same time, she knew you'd blame her and hate her if she said no." Finally, her eyes met his. They still glistened with teary sadness. "Brady, she knows about us. She didn't say, but I can tell. Did you tell her?"

He shook his head. "No! I wouldn't want her to hate you. And... and it would hurt her too much to think one of her friends is betraying her."

"That's my point. I'd never betray her. And I do believe she's got Oliver's best interests at heart. She's dead set on winning the Top Mom spot. In fact, I told her..." She shrugged. "I told her that if they offered it to me, I'd turn it down and recommend her instead. I can't think of anyone who wants it more." She shook her head. "Because she thinks it will make you love her again."

"That's ridiculous! It won't. You know that."

"My point is that she wants you so badly that she'll jump through any hoops to salvage what she had...*has* with you."

She picked up her purse. "The least you can do is meet her halfway."

Nothing she could say would have him agree with her. Any argument to the contrary would convince her that they should never see each other again.

Don't show your hand, he warned himself.

"I appreciate your honesty, Ally. Send me the pie shop prospectus. I'll read it immediately. If I like it, you'll have your funding within forty-eight hours. No strings attached." He knocked back the last of his scotch. "It'll be a pleasure doing business with you."

CHAPTER TEN

Wednesday, 13 February

"You're brilliant," Ally whispered to Jillian. "And not just in the filling and crust department, either. Look at all the children! They've never been so quiet...or so busy!"

She was right. For the children's Valentine's Day party, PHM&T had rented out the Presidio Golf Club's clubhouse and Jillian had turned it into a pink heart-filled palace.

The *ooohs* and *ahhhs* of the other moms were all the proof she needed that she'd impressed them.

Well, most of them. "It's Pepto-Bismol pink! No, wait... More the hue of the inner labia," Mallory sniffed. "Thank goodness it doesn't smell like one."

Jillian winced when she heard that.

Ally patted her friend on the back. "Don't let her ruin your success." To Mallory, she called out, "Are you sure about that? I could have sworn it's darker. Please check your facts. If you need one, I'll lend you my compact."

Mallory's face turned dark red.

"You know, I'm guessing *that's* its real color." Ally snapped open her compact in Mallory's face.

Jillian was laughing so hard, she almost choked.

What impressed the mothers most were the numerous activities Jillian had devised to keep the children busy. Using heart-shaped cookie cutters, the Fivesies were creating bite-sized sandwiches of cheese and turkey slices. At the same time, each of the Foursies were decorating five-slotted shoe boxes with glitter, doilies and stamp pads, which would serve as mailboxes for the Valentines being created by the Threesies.

Valentines and boxes were to be auctioned off, purchased with chocolates. Mounds represented one hundred dollars, Peanut Butter cups were worth five hundred dollars, and Hershey's Kisses were a thousand dollars.

"Why not pennies, nickels and dimes?" Jade asked Kimberley.

Kimberley's thin brow arched high enough to almost hit her forehead. "Are you kidding? Bettina never passes up an opportunity to have the children learn the value of a dollar. Or a thousand dollars, for that matter." She licked her lips. "The auction was my idea. I figure the sooner they discern good art from bad, the better. Like that monstrosity over there!"

She pointed to a forlorn-looking shoebox topped with

fifteen ripped strips of black construction paper. Sad stick figures were painted on the sides.

Jade didn't have the heart to tell her new bestie that it was the handiwork of her four-year-old son, Titus.

Why rock the boat? Jade asked herself. *She's so sweet! She's giving me a dozen leads for my AP class. And besides, she's already told me she thinks I should be Top Mom.*

Jade suspected she already had Bettina's vote, too, what with the money Brady gave Art to invest for him. Still, she was paranoid that Bettina was the type who checked her husband's cell phone ID. If so, surely she'd know he had called her.

And that he was still calling, in fact. Why couldn't he just leave her alone?

As for the other three committee members, none of them made it a point to warm up to her. Votes for Lorna was a given, considering her relationship to Bettina. As for Sally, she always smiled when she was around Ally. Joanna seemed to like her, too.

Jade could tell Mallory didn't like anyone. Maybe that worked in her favor, but she doubted it.

&

THE TWOSIES' MOMS WERE TO RUN THE AUCTION. EACH TIME A bid was made on a box, one of the children would be allowed to hit the toddler-sized podium with a rubber mallet.

The Onesies were in charge of the "bank." Each Onesie

was given five tulle bags filled with loose chocolates, to hand out to the older children.

Everything was running smoothly until the auction began. Suddenly Mallory's son, Angus, pointed under one of the tables and yelled at the top of his lungs, "Hey! One of the babies is eating all the chocolates!"

All heads dropped under the table.

The culprit was Zoe. The proof was smeared all over her lips.

She wasn't alone. Amelia and Addison had followed her lead, tearing open the bags and popping the chocolates into their mouths.

Angus grabbed one of the bags out of Zoe's hand. "I'm not letting you eat mine!"

In retaliation, Zoe bit him on the arm.

Yelping, Angus stood straight up and banged his head on the tabletop.

"My son! He's been attacked by your brat," Mallory screamed at Ally.

The children lunged at any Onesie in sight, even the obedient ones. Horrified, the Onesies cried at the top of their lungs as the bags were ripped from their pudgy little fingers.

The mothers coming to their children's aid were just as bad. The Onesies' mommies clasped their terrified babies to their breasts, while the moms of the older children insisted that their children were only taking what was rightfully theirs.

Tossing a twin under each arm, Jillian worked her way out of the free-for-all. Ally and Lorna with howling children in tow, were right on her heels. They made it to the front door—

Only to find it blocked by Bettina.

Was there a scowl on her face? It was hard to tell, considering the smoothness of her brow. But the tone of her voice left no doubt otherwise. "Jillian, dear, if this is what you call 'fun and games,' I can only imagine the kind of board member you'd make! In fact—"

A phone went off, but the ringtone, "*How Much Is That Doggie in the Window*," was nothing any of the Onesies moms had on their cells.

Bettina's eyes grew as wide as her eyelid blepharoplasty would allow. "Emergency! I must take this!" She turned her back on the others, all of whom realized there was an apt metaphor in that.

"You mean....my baby is here? Oh my God! I'll be right over!"

All the others exchanged puzzled glances. *Was Bettina adopting a child?*

God help the poor child...

When she turned to face them, Bettina's smile was luminous. Girlish almost. "I must leave immediately! Lorna, be a doll and do me the favor of taking Lily with you, okay?"

"Sure," Lorna murmured. "Bettina I...I don't know what to say except—I'm so proud you're so openhearted." She gave her sister-in-law a hug.

Stunned, touched in fact, Bettina patted her shoulder. "Lorna... thank you for understanding. Lily is very excited about it too, of course. I just hope they get along. If not, the little beggar will be confined to the terrace, I guess."

Ally, Lorna and Jillian exchanged shocked looks. Twenty stories up?

Bettina was already halfway down the sidewalk before she turned back around. "And, Jillian dear, great party! Just make sure to clean up the mess. Ask Mallory for her help."

Ally and Lorna had to prop Jillian up before she dropped the twins.

Jillian smiled and nodded, but she waited until Bettina hopped in her car and drove off before muttering through her smile, "Like hell I will." She turned to Ally. "Quid pro quo. If you'll help with cleanup, I'll help set up the adult party tomorrow night. "

Ally shook her head adamantly "Um…no, no, nothing to worry about. Got it covered! Feel free to take the night off."

"Really? Don't you want me to—?"

Ally's way of changing the subject was to wave in the direction of the ruckus. "Shouldn't we clean up Armageddon?"

Suddenly Jillian's face turned white. "Oh, heck! When the fight broke out, two of the Fivesies boys were eating glue! I've got to get back in there!"

"I'm on it. Go clear out the rest of the troops." Lorna shook her head. "If their mothers ask, I'll tell them the boys are high on sugar. *Just*…sugar."

&

THE PUPPY WAS A BITCH.

No! Bettina thought horrified. *This is wrong, all wrong!*

And it was so puny, too. Plain black, like a gutter rat! Nothing at all like big, strong, and deep auburn Caligula.

Sybil was in the process of ingratiating herself to a man who was buying two of the puppies, not exactly the ideal time for Bettina to tap her on the shoulder, but she did so anyway.

Bettina shook her head at Sybil. "This will not do! You knew I wanted a male."

"Sorry, but I can't predict the sex of the pups. As it turns out, this litter's pick was a big strapping male, and a female is the runt. Life goes on. Take her or leave her."

"In that case, I'll leave her," Bettina sneered.

Sybil shrugged. "Bu-bye! Don't let the dog door hit you on the way out." She turned back to the man.

Bettina was mortified at the thought, but more so by Sybil's assumption that she would be leaving empty-handed. She tapped Sybil on the shoulder again. "Aren't you forgetting something?"

Sybil turned back to her, confused. "I beg your pardon?"

"I'd like my check back."

"Sorry, no refunds." She pointed to the sign over the door.

"But...it was ten thousand dollars!"

"And you've refused to take the puppy you bought. That's not my fault. It wasn't a deposit, it was a purchase."

"But you said you had a waiting list for the pup, so there

is no loss to you! And besides, it's a thoroughbred and will find a home with someone who will love her."

Sybil walked Bettina toward the door. "Speaking of dog lovers, the new owners for the pick have arrived. Time for you to skedaddle."

This time she shoved Bettina out the door, and locked it behind her.

How dare she!

I'll sue, Bettina fumed. *I'll fight her in every court in California! I'll*—

A woman tapped her on the shoulder. "Excuse me. You're Bettina Connaught-Cross, aren't you?" She stuttered the question in a hushed, reverent tone, then backed away slightly, wrapping her arm around her husband.

Both were young, happy, and....

Pregnant.

Perfect, thought Bettina.

She lifted her head and deigned them with a regal smile. "Yes, I am. So nice to meet you, Mrs. and Mr...." She paused, and tilted her head in what she hoped gave off the impression of true interest.

"I'm Candy McIntosh, and this is my husband, Richard." She pushed him forward a bit. "We—I mean, I'll soon be applying for PHM&T, as you can see." She patted her belly gently.

Bettina clapped her hands in mock glee. "How joyous! A boy, or a girl?"

"Girl," the proud father-to-be piped in. "We're due in April."

"How wonderful! And all the more so, because you are also Tibetan mastiff lovers!" Then her smile faded. "What a shame! From the applicants we've already received for your birth year of Onesies, the girls are outnumbering the boys two to one."

The woman blanched. The glimmer of hope died in her eyes.

"I am *so* sorry! But the good news is you'll have your wonderful little puppy to console your baby. And it will grow into a superior watch dog. A godsend, considering the company your baby will be keeping in some of those other playgroups. Sadly, my own little girl—Lily, only four—won't be getting the sweet boy puppy she'd hoped for."

Bettina felt a tear in her eye. *I'm* crying? *What an odd sensation…*

The woman patted Bettina's arm sympathetically.

To Bettina's delight, she was able to squeeze out yet another tear. Seeing it peek out from under Bettina's long lashes, the woman motioned her husband to one side.

Their whispered discussion was heated, but short. Bettina caught the words, "…feel so sorry for her…" from the wife, and "…make a deal…" from the husband.

"How mortifying!" the wife hissed back. "Why, she'd be insulted—"

"Excuse me," Bettina interjected. "I couldn't help overhearing. And yes, I'd be honored to accept your male pup…" She paused. "And I'm just as honored to champion your application to our application committee."

The wife's fist pump was a bit déclassé, but Bettina

forgave it in light of what she was to receive in return: total domination.

To her mind, admission to PHM&T was a fair trade.

❦

"LILY, DEAR, COME DOWN HERE, QUICKLY! HE'S COME! YOU'RE little prince has arrived!"

The leitmotif of Tchaikovsky's *Swan Lake Ballet*, wafting from Lily's second-floor room, suddenly went silent. A moment later Lily was running down the grand staircase. "A prince—*here*? Where, Mummy? Where?"

Bettina held up the furry auburn puppy with both hands, as if he were the successor to the lion king. "Here my darling! Let me introduce you to Prince Vsevolod Ivanovich!"

Lily stopped mid-way on the stairs to stare at the little bundle of fur squirming in her mother's arm.

From the disappointed look on her face, her mother realized this was not the prince her daughter was expecting.

Also not anticipated was the warm stream of urine trickling out of the puppy and down Bettina's arm, baptizing her brand new Joseph Altuzarra striped linen blazer.

She screamed as she dropped the puppy on the foyer's plush Oriental rug. It whined mournfully as it scurried off for cover in the direction of Art's study.

Good, Bettina thought. *I hope it takes a crap in there.*

From Art's angry shout a few moments later, she guessed it had done just that.

Lily stared at her mother, mortified. "Mummy, whatever made you think I wanted a dog? I like cats. Oh, and ponies, too!" Shaking her head in dismay, she flew back up the staircase, slamming her bedroom door behind her.

Bettina collapsed on the rug, weeping. The *Pas de Deux* commenced again. It was fitting background music for her despair. More importantly, it drowned out her sobs.

She had wanted Prince Vsevolod to be the surprise love of Lily's life.

No, in truth *she* wanted to be the love of Lily's life. She wanted Lily to adore and revere *her*.

She wanted Art's love and admiration as well.

Once, a long time ago, she presumed he did love her. Had she only imagined that? Maybe he had never loved her. Maybe he had only married her for her money.

She buried her head in her hands.

"Bettina, what the hell were you thinking?"

She looked up to find Art standing over her. He was holding Prince Vsevolod Ivanovich by the scruff of the pup's neck.

How dare he.

"Put him down. *Now.*" Her tone was low and menacing.

Art hesitated, but did as he was told. The puppy trembled, but stayed put.

"Now, down on all fours!" Bettina's command left no doubt she meant business.

Both the dog and Art looked at her uncomprehendingly. "Bettina, I don't think—"

"You're right, Art. *You don't think.*" She rose to her feet.

"If you had half a brain, you would never have had an affair with Kelly. Or any number of other women, too, I presume."

The accusation hit its mark. He dropped his head in shame.

Then he dropped to his knees as commanded.

She kicked off a kitten-heel pump.

Her whack was so hard that it dropped him on his elbows.

With the second hit, he fell over.

She bent down and murmured, "Resume the position...again."

He nodded slowly. "I think...I think it would be wise if we had a safety word."

"Okay, sure." Bettina thought for a moment. "It will be Prince Vsevolod."

He winced. "That's a bit wordy. How do you spell it, anyway?"

His impertinence earned him another whack.

Then another, and another, until he was groaning in pain.

Or was it pleasure?

When he pulled her onto the rug beside him, she had her answer.

His kiss was so deep she was lightheaded.

She was aroused.

She pushed him off, but she didn't hit him again.

In truth, she couldn't. The kitten heel had flown off.

Should I suggest we go into the bedroom and make love? She wondered.

No, she couldn't. Not with Lily awake and on the same floor.

Not in the bed where Kelly's ghost taunted her.

Fuck Kelly.

And fuck Art, too. But not tonight.

I'll make him beg for it, she vowed.

Right then and there she realized her shoe budget was going to go through the roof.

And for once, Art wouldn't complain about it.

CHAPTER ELEVEN

Thursday, 14 February

"CHRISTIAN HATES ME, DOESN'T HE?" ALLY MURMURED TO Barry as she straightened his tuxedo bowtie.

"Yes, dear. So sorry, but it's true. But if it's any consolation, he hates me even more. After all, I should be spending Valentine's Day with him, alone. Instead, I gave in to you." Barry shrugged, but kept the smile on his face, so that anyone observing them would presume their hosts were congratulating each other for pulling off a fabulous gathering.

Christian is upstairs babysitting Zoe while the love of his life is playing my beard, Ally thought. "I'm so sorry, Barry. Once again I've let the club get in the way of our real lives."

Barry smiled. "I'm hoping your pie idea takes off like gangbusters, so that you're too busy for all this silliness." He wrapped his arm around her. "Don't worry about Christian. He took a whole bottle of champagne upstairs with him. Now that Zoe is asleep, I'm sure he's watching *Revenge* reruns and drowning his sorrows in a 1995 Clos Du Mesnil." He looked out at the crowd. "By the way, dear, you were right! Remove the folding doors between our two living rooms, and we've got an instant ballroom."

All evening long, the fifty PHM&T members and their husbands flowed easily through the large, open space. The caterers had set up a bar in one of the kitchens and prepared tasty appetizers in the other, which were offered on trays by waiters dressed in tuxedos and red bowties.

Pink, red and silver heart-shaped balloons filled with helium covered every inch of the eleven-foot ceilings of the classic Victorian. The golden glow of the tiny votive candles that filled a ceiling-high glass bookcase was doubled by the mirrored wall behind it. A fortune teller, dressed as the Queen of Hearts, gave readings of palms and tarot cards. Ally had coerced an old school chum, the Los Angeles-based jazz crooner Andrée Belle, to fly up for the event. As the petite and slender blonde sat atop Barry's baby grand piano, couples danced to her sultry renditions of Cole Porter love songs.

It's a perfect party for anyone in love, Ally thought sadly.

She tried hard not to glance over at Jade and Brady, who were chitchatting with Bettina, Art, Matt, Lorna and Jillian. Ally could tell Jillian was just as miserable. Since the PHM&T board presumed she was married to Scott, Caleb could not be by her side.

Since Brady's cash infusion into Life of Pie, Jillian and Ally had found the perfect retail space, in Pacific Heights' Union Street. Last week, while their daughters slept in their strollers and the two women surveyed the handiwork of the carpenter who had put in the counters and display shelves, Jillian broke down and admitted she and Caleb were no longer seeing each other.

"He insists I still love Scott." She had sobbed quietly.

Ally had put her arm around her friend. "Do you feel there's any truth in that?"

At first Jillian shook her head adamantly. But the shakes slowed into a shrug before she nodded once, half-heartedly. "I can't help it. Despite Scott's duplicity, I still feel the break-up was just as much my fault as his. There are always telltale signs. If I'd picked up on them instead of focusing so much on the house and…and…"

"And your daughters?" Ally had turned her friend's head until they were eye to eye. "Scott is supposedly a smart guy. My goodness, he should have been able to express his feelings to his wife of ten years! If he didn't want children, he should have said so upfront. If he was disappointed because the children you had were twin girls, he should still man up and accept them for who they are, his own flesh and blood."

Jillian sighed. "If only he believed they were truly his. And that's the problem. He still believes they're Jeff's."

Ally shooed that notion away with a flip of her wrist. "He's just trying to get out of alimony. Well, the good news is that the success of the pie shop means you won't need him or his money."

Jillian snorted. "Trust me. I'll still need a man. Hey, a girl has needs, you know. And Caleb...well, let me put it this way—he completes me."

Yes, Ally knew, all too well the need for that one special relationship.

The desire to feel a man by her side.

How she longed to hold Brady. To kiss him and have him make love to her.

And now, as their eyes met across a crowded room, as the dancers shuffled and kissed to Andrée's sultry rendition of "Night and Day," she could tell he was thinking the same thing.

Someday perhaps, she promised him silently.

Had he nodded or was that her imagination?

To force herself out of her pleasant trance, she squeezed Barry's hand tightly. "Come on, it's time to liven up this party with a game of Covert Cupid."

He sighed. "Salacious party favors from one frustrated housewife to another? The excitement is palpable."

She tweaked his nose. "Don't be such a spoil sport! Just bring in the damn gift basket. By the way, with Jillian's permission, I've rigged the game so that she draws the prize I donated, a trip to a B&B in Mendocino. If it works, she's already promised to give it back to me. It's my thank-you present to you and Christian."

"Wow thanks, Allycat! I just hope he sobers up before the expiration date," he laughed. "Well, let the games begin!"

❧

Who the hell is Brady mooning over? Kimberley wondered. It certainly isn't Jade. For the past hour, she's been cornered by that horndog, Art. Is it the singer? *Why, I'll strangle that little hussy—*

No, his gaze went even farther across the room.

He was staring at Ally Thornton.

Ha! What a jerk he is. Kimberley smirked. *He won't have a snowball's chance in hell of getting her in bed. Just look at all the love pats she's giving her husband, Barry. And the way she tweaks his nose, the way he laughs at the joke she's whispering in his ear. I could be shouting at the top of my lungs and my Jerry still wouldn't turn around.*

She watched as Ally's husband walked to the foyer table. As he hoisted the Covert Cupid gift basket, she sighed with relief. Finally!

Her own cat-and-mouse torture came in a very small package. She made sure that she'd pulled Jade's name, but the gift was strictly for Brady.

When Jade opens it, all hell will break loose between her and Brady. Kimberley smirked. *She'll be seeing red.*

How very appropriate for Valentine's Day.

❧

Jade was only listening half-heartedly to the giggles and guffaws coming from the crowd as each club member opened the gift from their Covert Cupid. Most of the items were silly: peignoirs, fuzzy pink handcuffs, a bunny tail and floppy ears.

And lots of Viagra.

It reminded Jade of all props on the set of her porn flick, *Alice in Wonderlust.*

She blushed at the thought. *Oh no,* she thought in horror. *What if someone here gets my movie as a gag gift?*

She glanced around at the laughing crowd. No one was watching her. No one knew.

Relief surged through her. *I've got to quit thinking about the past and work toward the future,* she vowed. *My future, with Brady and Oliver.*

Her conversation with Ally had put her mind at ease. Despite the obvious attraction Brady had for her friend, Jade knew all too well that it took two to tango.

At the children's holiday party, when Jade had run into her movie costar, Ally had seen her lose her cool. But Ally had been enough of a friend to assure her that their friendship meant more than ratting her out.

Ally had also promised she'd never let Brady's attraction get in the way of her friendship. But isn't that exactly what happened when Ally kissed Brady on New Year's Eve?

From then on, she knew Ally couldn't be trusted.

The best advice she ever got from anyone had come from the movie's director. "Timing is everything," he had said.

He had been talking about her costar's staying power. Still, Jade realized it applied to a variety of situations.

Like when Ally came to Jade after the Onesie's reading time and asked her if she'd mind if Brady joined Bracknell's corporate board, Jade's heart almost quit beating. She knew it would give Brady exactly what he wanted—more time with Ally.

She also realized he'd always resent her if she said no to Ally. After Art's blackmail attempt, Brady was one step away from banishing her from Oliver's life. She couldn't afford to give him another reason to do so.

When Ally swore again that she'd do nothing to damage their friendship, she had no choice but to say yes. Perhaps it was the perfect test of Ally's loyalty after all. If Ally failed, Jade would let Bettina know.

Bettina would banish Ally and Zoe from the club. And Ally would hate Brady for disgracing her and her little girl.

All the way around, it was a win-win situation.

As fate would have it, she'd drawn Ally's name for Covert Cupid. Her gift to her frenemy was a heart-shaped mirror. She had it inscribed with a phrase she'd found on Brainy Quotes, accredited to Sophocles:

Trust dies, but mistrust blossoms.

Every time she looks at herself, she'll think of me, not him, Jade thought.

At least, she hoped so. Brady wasn't easy to forget.

So why did she find him so easy to forgive?

Kimberley nudged her back to reality. "Silly, Jade! Your name was called! Go up and get your gift."

Jade nodded and pushed her way through the crowd until she was at Barry's side.

"Here you go, doll," he said with a wink. "It was really addressed to Brady, but we both know he's got the wrong equipment for PHM&T membership. It's too tiny to be a cattle prod, but if you're lucky, maybe it's a choke leash."

He knows Brady too well, she thought sadly.

She ripped open the packet. Inside was a purple thong.

Just like the one she found in her cabinet on Thanksgiving.

The note said, *Dear Brady, Thinking of you! Again...and again...and again...*

Who the hell had pulled her name?

She stared out at the crowd. So, he was fucking one of them! One of her so-called friends.

But of course it had to be Ally. She'd been there, on Thanksgiving, without a date.

Without a husband.

She was the only one who could have put the thong in the cabinet.

And she acted so innocent when I asked her about it at the children's holiday party, Jade remembered. *What a fool I've been!*

The crowd roared, "Hold it up! Hold it up! Hold it up!"

As she did, she looked directly at Brady.

He turned white. He frowned as he stared back at her.

"Wow, Brady looks like he's seen a ghost," Kimberley whispered in her ear. "What's got him so wound up?"

Jade ignored her. She was too busy watching where Brady's eyes went next. She guessed he'd look at the prankster, his lover.

She was right. His eyes went directly to Ally, who was watching Jade intently.

She sees how upset I am, Jade reasoned. *I guess she's happy. She accomplished her goal.*

So, why did Ally look so concerned for her?

"Wow, Brady certainly looks guilty," Kimberley snickered. "Why do you think that is?"

Holding back her tears, Jade whispered, "Because he's having an affair with Ally Thornton."

❧

"WHAT?" KIMBERLEY COULDN'T BELIEVE HER EARS.

She looked from Brady, to Ally, and back again.

Why, that son of a bitch!

Why, that bitch.

So, that's who he's two-timing me with…

Kimberley tried to get a hold of herself. Still, her voice shook when she asked, "I'm…I'm so sorry, Jade. But…are you sure? How do you know?"

Jade's fake smile hid the sadness in her voice. "He told me so. But up until now I've given her the benefit of the doubt that she hasn't…that she hasn't given into her own feelings about him. Now I know she's been lying." She lowered her head. "She better watch her back."

Kimberley looked at her sharply. "What do you mean by that?"

Jade started to say something, but then thought better of it. "Nothing. I'm just…upset." She leaned her head on Kimberley's shoulder. "Thank you…for being my friend."

Kimberley smiled as she patted Jade's head. *Good,* she thought. *Brady's looking at us. Serves him right.*

At this point, Kimberley reasoned, *even if Ally had not succumbed to Brady's charms, Jade certainly wouldn't believe her. And I'll warn Ally to leave him alone, or risk a scandal.*

Then Ally will tell Brady to take a hike, Kimberley thought gleefully. The last thing she needs is a threat to her club membership, let alone her marriage.

And with Jade watching his every move, Brady certainly wasn't going to rock the boat now.

Good. I've got him right where I want him—frustrated and horny.

She stroked Jade's arm. "You know what you need? A drink." She snapped her fingers at a waiter passing with a tray of champagne flutes.

What a perfect way to celebrate the end of Brady's next conquest!

Perhaps soon she would be celebrating the end of his marriage, too.

CHAPTER TWELVE

Friday, 15 February

ALL NIGHT LONG, JADE TOSSED AND TURNED IN HER BED IN THE guest room.

She knew what she had to do if she were to salvage the life she now lived and loved so much. If she were to salvage any chance she had to reconcile with Brady.

She woke up early and got dressed in her tightest designer jeans and a sheer top that showed off her fabulous breasts. The moment she heard Oliver talking gibberish to his favorite teddy bear, she went to get him.

As was his habit, he squealed whenever she came into his room. Quickly, she picked him up and shushed him with a finger to her smiling lips. She would never let him know when her heart was breaking, ever, for as long as she lived.

She strolled him out of the house, down toward Chestnut

Street, and into the Grove cafe, where she ordered scrambled eggs and a bagel to split with Oliver. She knew she was turning heads. She was used to that. Too bad Brady wasn't there to see how much she was admired.

Soon he'd appreciate her again. But first, Ally needed to make good on her promise to leave Brady alone.

If not, she'd make Ally's life a living hell. At least, as long as Ally was a member of PHM&T.

Now Kimberley knows that Ally is chasing after my husband, I have a protector on the Top Mom committee, Jade reasoned. *For that matter, Bettina will bend over backward for me, too, now that Art is handling Brady's money. One word from me and Ally is out of there.*

But before she started World War III, she'd read Ally the riot act.

She'd do it today during the meet-up.

She always fought better on a full stomach.

⁊⁊

JADE WAITED UNTIL THE OTHER ONESIES MOTHERS WERE SAFELY ensconced in the Marina Theater, where all of PHM&T groups had congregated for a special showing of the latest *Despicable Me* sequel before motioning Ally to follow her into the lobby.

As they made their way up the theater aisle, Kimberley turned around and gave Jade a thumbs-up sign.

Jade nodded at her. It was great to have a real friend like Kimberley.

During the admission competition, everyone had stuck together. If push came to shove and Ally ended their friendship, she wondered if Jillian would side with Ally now that they were in business together. And for that matter would Jade lose Lorna's friendship as well? She hoped not.

But when it came to the club, Lorna's friendship paled in comparison to Bettina's. And anyone with eyes in their head could see there was no love lost between the sisters-in-law.

Jade planned on being on the winning side. It was the only way she'd hold onto Brady.

"What's up?" Ally asked distractedly. She had every right to be, considering Zoe was banging on the theater's candy case, squealing for Milk Duds.

"Did you think I wouldn't get your sick little joke?"

"A joke?" Ally scooped up Zoe before turning to face her friend. "Jade, what are you talking about?"

"This!" Jade pulled out the purple thong and threw it at her. "Ally, I know it came from you."

Ally stared down at it. "Seriously, I don't know what the heck you're talking about."

"I was watching Brady! It was an anonymous gift, but he knew who gave it to me. And guess what? *He looked right at you when I held it up.*"

Ally blushed. "Whether he was looking at me or not, I had nothing to do with…this!"

"You mean to tell me you didn't leave one just like this in my kitchen cupboard—on Thanksgiving?"

Ally's jaw dropped open. "Are you *crazy?*"

Jade's glare was all Ally needed to see that she was very serious.

Ally took a deep breath. "Jade, I swear on my life. It wasn't me."

Jade shook her head in disbelief. Tears fell from her eyes onto the planes of her high cheekbones. "I must be going crazy. No, I—I'm just tired of being lied to." She looked at Ally. "There's nothing I can do about the fact Brady is sitting on your board or that he's investing in your new venture with Jillian. You asked my permission, I said yes. But now, it's time for you to keep your end of the bargain. If you're truly my friend, you'll leave him alone."

She didn't wait for Ally's answer.

She was glad it was dark in the theater. She didn't want anyone to see she was crying.

CHAPTER THIRTEEN

Tuesday, 29 February

"So, how about buying me a drink? That way, you can fill me in on the progress of Life of Pie." Brady could tell Ally was disappointed that he'd caught up with her in the Bracknell parking lot. Well, too bad. He missed her terribly.

Since the Valentine's party, she'd been avoiding him, and he couldn't figure out why. She still answered his emails, but without the usual familiarity he'd come to know. And she never answered his calls. Instead, she'd text back, using either Zoe or the pie shop's grand opening as her excuse to make any correspondence between short and sweet.

She hesitated, then shook her head. "I've got to get home and relieve the babysitter."

"Liar. Zoe is with Barry and Christian. I passed them in the park on my way over here."

She shrugged. "Okay, you caught me in a fib. I'm hoping I don't do the same with you."

His smile disappeared. "You won't. Ask me anything."

She took a deep breath. "Are you having an affair with someone?"

He laughed until he saw she wasn't joking. "Why would you say something like that?"

She reached into her purse and pulled out the purple thong. "I don't think Jade found this funny, either. In fact, she accused me of leaving one just like it at your house, on Thanksgiving, and then making this her Covert Cupid joke."

Brady stared down at it, but he didn't say a word.

Ally sighed. "Brady, whose is it?"

He blinked twice. Game over. Time to come clean.

He took a deep breath. "It belongs to Kimberley Savitch."

It was Ally's turn to be silent. Finally she whispered, "When?"

"It started before the Onesies admission. She was an easy mark. I was hoping she'd be an advocate for Oliver's admittance. She was. But when I asked Jade to come back so that Oliver could hold onto his place, I made it clear we needed to cool it."

"So that Jade wouldn't find out." Ally waited for him to validate the premise.

"Yes. And…and because by then I'd met you."

Ally nodded slowly. "Thank you for your honesty. I have to say, Brady Pierce, you are one conniving son of a bitch."

He shrugged. "Does that make me any more lovable?"

Ally couldn't hide her smile. "It barely makes you

human." Her smile faded as she added, "I don't think we can go on like this anymore."

"Do I disgust you?"

Ally nodded. "Yes. I'm sorry, but knowing how you used Kimberley—"

He snorted loudly. "Used…her? My God, when I told her we should cool it, she tried to blackmail me! I called her bluff."

"And she called Jade's. Obviously, she was Jade's Covert Cupid. And obviously Jade is upset over this. Do you know how close the two of them have become? Brady, for your own sake, you need to put her in her place!"

"I thought I had." He leaned against the car. "I wasn't counting on her airing her dirty laundry in public, literally."

"Threaten to air it for her. Threaten to expose her to Bettina. The club is Kimberley's life. If it's known that she's been chasing after another woman's husband, she'll be kicked out."

"My God, Ally, you're a genius. Game, set, match!"

Without thinking, he reached to kiss her. Stunned, she pulled away. Holding her hand to her mouth, she muttered, "Don't you ever do that again."

She fumbled in her purse for her car's electronic key. But it was crammed with so many of Zoe's Lego Duplo blocks that she couldn't find it. Cursing, she crouched down and turned the purse upside down on the sidewalk.

When finally she found the key, she clicked it and jumped into the car.

"I'm keeping my promise to Jade, and to myself," Ally said.

She drove off, leaving the Legos behind.

Frustrated with himself, Brady kicked the plastic blocks. When they scattered, one hit his car hard enough that the alarm went off.

CHAPTER FOURTEEN

Friday, 1 March

BRADY'S CALL ASKING HER TO MEET HIM AT THE LUCKY 13 IN
the Duboce Triangle had Kimberley walking on a cloud all
day. She easily talked Sally Dunder into taking her tots for
an overnight. Sally owed her a sitter exchange for all the
times she twisted the arms of PHM&T members to pull their
weight—or at least pull a few weeds—in the community
garden.

The Lucky13 was a dive. She had expected nothing more.
In fact, the seedier the better. It made the meeting so
thrillingly clandestine!

She wondered if Brady had met Jade in a place like this.
The women lounging around the bar could easily pass for
her clan. They were all low-rent skanks.

If that's what rang his chimes, she could role-play, no

problem. Usually she bought her lingerie at Chadwick's on Chestnut or Les Cent Culottes on Polk in Russian Hill. This time, though, before their rendezvous, she drove over to the Ross Dress for Less on Bay Street and bought a leopard print push up bra and a matching thong. The price tag, just eight ninety-nine, seemed too good to be true. She wondered if it was used. She shuddered at the thought that she might catch something, but put them on anyway in a dressing room that had no doors, not even a curtain. Talk about low rent.

Perfect.

In fact, she hoped the hotel room they'd end up in was just as gross as the bar and the Ross. One of her favorite fantasies of all time was that scene in *Monster's Ball* where Heath Ledger and Halle Berry made love standing up in front of the mirror. There were a more than a few just like it on the blocks surrounding the Lucky 13. In hindsight, standing up to fuck was the only option she'd give Brady. The last thing she needed to bring home with her was bedbugs. Her oldest son had been infected with head lice once, and it had freaked her out. Authenticity was good, but only up to a point.

The place was so dark that it had taken her a full five minutes to realize Brady was already sitting at the bar. When she saw he'd spotted her too, he motioned her to a booth in the corner, then excused himself from the two old men who were bending his ear, taking his pint of dark beer with him.

He dodged her kiss. "I'm going to make this short and sweet," he said. "Stay away from Jade. I don't care what excuse you give her. You can tell her she has bad breath for all I care. If you don't, I'll tell her the thong belongs to you. I'll also tell Bettina Connaught-Cross that we had a thing."

His attack stunned her at first. Then slowly anger filled the emptiness he left. "You wouldn't dare," she muttered.

He downed his beer. "Try me, Kimberley. You see, you've left me no choice. Jade loves me. She may hate the fact that I don't love her back, but she's made her choice." He leaned in close. "Can you say the same? Will your husband stand by you? And if Jade is angry enough to tell Bettina you voted for me because we were fucking, do you think you'll be asked to stick around?"

Everything he said was right.

They both knew it.

If Bettina found out, she'd be a pariah. She'd be known as the club skank. No, just a run-of-the-mill skank, because she'd no longer be in the club.

Kimberley pursed her lips.

Then she stood up, picked up Brady's beer, and flung it in his face.

She could not run to her car fast enough. A bum, sitting in a broken Barcalounger, whistled as she hustled past him. She felt as if he could see right through her. Or at least, as close up as her leopard skin bra and panties.

The moment she got into her house, she locked the front door and stripped off all her clothes. But she didn't toss them in the dirty clothes hamper. Instead, she put them in the garbage can, tying the scented plastic bag tight in case she was right about the bugs.

Then she jumped into the shower and scrubbed her skin until it was raw.

She went to bed naked and cried herself to sleep.

She expected Jerry to get home late.

She guessed he wouldn't even notice she had no clothes on.

She was right on both counts.

CHAPTER FIFTEEN

Thursday, March 21

SOMETHING IS CLEARLY WRONG, JADE THOUGHT.

She had every right to be paranoid. For over a month now, Kimberley had been dodging her. Whenever she phoned for a playdate or to grab a cup of coffee to go over some AP class ideas, the call would roll over to Kimberley's voice mail. If she tried to chat up Kimberley after their meet-ups, her friend was polite, but definitely frosty, and she always had somewhere else to be right that very moment.

As luck would have it, she ran into Kimberley at the Golden Gate Valley library's Tales and Tots reading hour. In a final desperate attempt to find out why she was being ignored, Jade edged her way through the thick crowd, plop-ping Oliver down next to Kimberley and her two little ones.

She gave her friend a big smile. "Wow, imagine meeting you here!"

Kimberley blanched then glanced around furtively. If Jade didn't know better, she'd think Kimberley was on the lam.

Not able to stand it any longer, Jade came right out with it. "Hey, are you're avoiding me?"

Kimberley's smile quivered. "Who, me? No! I've just... The board is *so* busy right now, what with vetting the AP class proposals and all."

Jade bit her lip. "That's why I've been calling you. I'm freaking out about mine. None of the leads you've given me have panned out. The concert violinist was already asked to participate with the Foursies by Gwen. And the Cubist painter was called by Marcia, so he's already onboard to work with the Threesies. Even that long shot—you know, the VIP soccer dude from Manchester, England—was asked by Hillary to work with the Twosies!" She sighed. "I'm always a day late and a dollar short."

"Poor you."

Jade looked up sharply, and just in time to catch the tail end of Kimberley's smirk before it faded. "Kimberley, I truly thought we were friends. Please be honest. Is there something you're not telling me?"

Kimberley's eyes narrowed. She opened her mouth to say something, but then thought better of it. Instead, she shrugged. "Yeah, well, you've got to be Johnny on the spot with these things. Time's running out, kiddo. All instructors' curricula vitae have to be submitted next week, along with a curriculum outline. And as for our friendship, Jade, here's the dealio. As long as this contest is going on, I can't show favoritism to anyone. I've already been called on the carpet for doing so."

"But Bettina likes me! I know she does!"

Kimberley's humorless laugh sent a chill up Jade's spine. "Yeah, and for all the right reasons, I'm guessing. Don't be so naïve, Jade. Don't you get it? You're the golden girl. As long as you watch your Ps and Qs, you'll be fine. Oh, and while you're at it, watch your back, too."

Pretending to be enthralled by the monotone storyteller, she turned her back to Jade.

Fine, Jade thought. *I can take a hint.*

She grabbed Oliver and stumbled over the floor filled with squirming tots until she reached the library's outer doors.

It was bright outside. The air was cold and brisk. *Good. I need some fresh air.*

She knew of a little pocket park just a block down at the corner of Gough and Green. It was grassy and had lots of benches, and there was always a dog or two. Running after any pups would keep Oliver busy while she thought through her next move.

She didn't see the man at first, but she heard him.

"It is not in the stars to hold our destiny, but in ourselves."

How beautiful and how true, Jade marveled. She turned around to see who had spoken to her.

The man was sitting on the sidewalk, up against the

corner market. His clothes were old and soiled. The soles of his shoes were open, exposing a big toe with a yellow nail. There was an empty vodka bottle at his side.

She just had to ask. "Did you just make that up?"

He tilted his head in her direction. His rheumy eyes scrutinized her from top to bottom. Liking what he saw, he smiled wide. He was missing a tooth in the back. "If I had, I'd be four hundred and fifty years old. It's from William Shakespeare's *Julius Caesar*. Cassius's lament to Brutus." He leaned forward toward Oliver's stroller, and chucked the tot under the chin. "Can you say it, little man? Go on, be Cassius."

Oliver gurgled something that sounded like "twawr."

Jade was thrilled. "Did you hear him? He said 'star.'"

The man shrugged. "It's possible. I was quoting the Bard before I could say my own last name, Pudberry." He held out a dirty hand. "Cornelius Reginald."

Jade took it slowly, and shook it gently. "Pierce. Jade. And this is Oliver."

"Ah! As in *Twist*, eh? Middling Copperfield, but the tykes find it relatable. We're all orphans, metaphorically speaking."

"I didn't learn any Shakespeare until I was in high school."

The man laughed. "Can you quote any now?"

Jade blushed and shook her head. "No. I guess I never made it a priority."

"Not you. But your parents. Our educational system and our society have let us all down." The man shook his head forlornly. "The ancient Greeks quoted Homer to their offspring. Shakespeare rolled trippingly off the tongues of wee Regents. Today, we leave our children in front of a television. Pray tell, what kind of vocabulary can they learn from a sponge who wears jodhpurs and has a starfish as a sidekick?" He rolled his eyes. "Blasphemy!"

He's right, Jade thought. *This bum has it all figured out.*

So, why is he a bum in the first place?

"What about your destiny?" she blurted out.

The man looked down on the concrete sidewalk. It was pocked and stained with soot and grease. Its gray hue had only one spot of color, a wad of bright blue Bubble Yum. "If you have a persistent drinking problem, a Nobel Prize in literature only takes you so far." Even as he hid his bottle to one side, he raised his head proudly. "Yes, that's right. I'm *that* Cornelius Reginald Pudberry."

"Oh!" Jade was awed. Why, if she scored a Nobel Prize winner for her AP instructor, she'd win the Top Mom slot hands down!

She opened her purse and pulled out a fifty-dollar bill. "I have a proposition for you."

His eyes got big when he noticed the denomination of the bill, but wariness shrank them back down to size. "Sorry, but the latest run on my sperm bank has cleaned me out."

Jade's face turned red. "Oh…No! I mean, I'm hoping you'll be free to teach a class once a week, granted your students will be somewhat on the younger side."

"Ack! High schoolers." Pudberry's annoyance came out in a long, deep sigh.

Jade shook her head. "No, not exactly."

"Middle schoolers?" He shrugged. "Their minds are still open. At least, they are in sixth grade. By eighth, hormones are raging."

She stuttered, "Quite frankly, I was thinking about five-year-olds."

"Ha!" He mulled that over for a moment. All the while, his eyes never left that fifty-dollar bill perched casually in Jade's hand.

"You said it yourself about the Greeks and all. So, why can't our kids be like theirs?"

"Well, in the first place, they don't speak Greek." He shrugged. "Still, it would be an interesting challenge." He leaned back, deep in thought. "A Shakespeare play in the first quarter, perhaps. Followed by something from Dickens. Then a Trollope. In the fourth quarter, maybe Galsworthy." He snatched the fifty-dollar bill from her hand.

She grabbed it back. "There are some conditions."

"Ah, Lady MacBeth are we?" When he threw back his head to chuckle, it slammed against the concrete wall. Rubbing it, he added, "'Look like an innocent flower, but be the serpent under 't' , eh?"

Jade frowned. "Maybe. But dig it. These moms will eat both of us alive if we don't deliver the goods. That means cleaning you up, inside and out. But I'll make it worth your while. A good wage, and"—she paused to steel herself—"I'll include room and board. But no booze. Okay?"

Pudberry looked down at the vodka bottle. He tossed it away. It clattered as it rolled down the sidewalk. "It's not a tenured position at Stanford, but I guess it will do in a pinch. Perhaps I'll use the experience as research for my next thesis. '*Litterarum puer prodigia.*'"

Jade stared down at him, awed. "Wow! Was that Greek?"

Once again he guffawed. And once again, his head hit the wall. "Latin, my dear girl. It means 'literary child prodigies.'"

Jade helped him up. "Either I've got to quit making you laugh, or I'll have to get smarter. Otherwise I'll give you a concussion."

He shook his head sadly. "If you get smarter, you may lose your charming sense of humor."

"Oh, I don't know about that. 'Stupid is as stupid does.'"

He looked at her in awe. "Did you just make that up?"

"Nah. Forrest Gump."

Pudberry nodded appreciatively. "I've got to sneak into the movies more often."

CHAPTER SIXTEEN

Sunday, 31 March

"WHERE ARE THE PINK AND BLUE TIE-DYED ONES?" LORNA looked frantically in the back of her SUV where two crates, holding eggs painted in a rainbow of colors, were still waiting to be hidden before the start of the PHM&T Easter Egg Extravaganza. "Oh my God! I'll bet we left them on the kitchen table at home! I knew we should have taken separate cars! I've got to go back and get them."

"Quit panicking," Matthew said softly. "Brady has already hidden them. He also got rid of the ugly lime green ones."

"Did he take the golden egg, too?"

"Nope. I hid that one myself. I found a really great spot. It'll be a miracle if anyone finds it."

Lorna wagged a finger. "You're not supposed to lose it, just make it harder to find than the others."

"Then I'd say the mission was accomplished." He grabbed her finger, using it to pull her closer so that he could give her a kiss. "So what are my marching orders?"

"We'll each take one of the last two crates. If I can find Jade, she can watch Dante with Oliver." She scanned the park. "Where is she, anyway?"

"She's over there, chatting up Bettina about her AP instructor. She wangled some Nobel Prize winner." He swung Dante onto his shoulders. "I'll walk our little man over there. It's time he met Bettina's puppy, anyway. " Seeing his wife's frown, he added, "Don't worry! Prince Whatever-His-Name-Is won't hurt him."

"I'm not worried about the puppy. I was thinking of Bettina. If she notices something doesn't seem right with Dante, she'll have Eleanor up in arms."

Matt frowned. "Let's just get it over with and tell everyone the truth."

"No! Not until...not until the results come back from this latest round of tests."

"But our therapist says we should get everything out in the open, with everyone who loves us. What are you afraid of?"

He wants everything out in the open? she thought. *Okay, here it is.* "The 'unconditional love' the Connaughts are famous for."

She had nothing more to say on the matter. From the resigned look on his face, neither did he.

She grabbed one of the cartons of eggs and handed it to him. "We better get moving. The park will be filled with tots in another thirty minutes. And take Dante off your shoulders. Around that puppy, he's better off in his stroller."

She took the other carton and started up the hill.

༃

"You've really outdone yourself, Jade. A Nobel Prize winner! How thrilling! And you're hosting him during his tenure, too? Wise move! What a wonderful dinner party guest he'll make!"

I wish Brady saw it that way, Jade thought.

Unfortunately, Brady had made it clear that offering "the Bum" (as he liked to call their guest) the au pair suite off the kitchen was begging for trouble. "Now I'll have to go out and get a lock for the liquor cabinet," he groused.

"C.R. promised to stay sober," she had reminded him. "So far, he's done everything I've asked of him."

Brady shrugged. He knew she had a point. After a bath, a shave, a decent haircut and some new duds, he almost looked the part of an egghead, albeit not one with a Nobel Prize hidden in his sock drawer.

"Yeah, okay, so far so good. But just remember, 'Promises are made to be broken.' That ain't Shakespeare, but I think in this case it's apropos."

"Brady, all I'm asking you to do is to give him a chance. If he doesn't work out, I'll drop him back where I found him."

Brady slammed out of the house.

Well, thank goodness Bettina is tickled pink, thought Jade. Then again, she wasn't the one who had walked in on Jade while she was combing lice out of C.R.'s hair.

"MY BAD, BAD BOY," BETTINA COOED AT PRINCE VSEVOLOD AS she leaned down to shoo him away from the pram. "If only Lily were a Fivesie! How I long to see her play Juliet! Well, perhaps next year."

Matthew rolled his eyes. "What? Not Viola?"

Bettina dismissed him with a shrug. "*Twelfth Night?* I should say not! There's no death scene. And Lily was born to play tragedy."

"Just like her mother," Matthew muttered under his breath. "Hey, Jade, would you mind watching Dante while I unload the last of the eggs?"

Jade smiled and nodded. "No problem! Ollie will love the company." She placed the strollers side-by-side, so the boys were closer.

Matthew waved as he walked back to the SUV.

Had he looked back, maybe he would've noticed that Jade hadn't locked the brake on Dante's stroller when she moved it closer to Oliver's.

A labrador retriever came over to sniff up Prince Vsevolod. The puppy, overwhelmed by the attention, nipped the retriever on the nose. The bigger dog's angry response was to bite back.

Bettina's mother tiger instinct kicked in, She shooed retriever away from Prince Vsevolod.

No one noticed that Dante's stroller had rolled down the hill until it was too late.

"Oh my God! Oh my God!" Bettina ran after it, but it was too fast for her. It toppled before it reached the sidewalk. Dante was flung into the grass. The way he was lying there, moaning but not moving, sent Bettina into a tizzy.

She picked him up and ran with him to her car.

"Watch Prince Vsevolod for me," she shouted to Jade. "Oh! And Lily, too!"

Luckily, the nearest emergency room, the one at California Pacific Medical Center, was just a few blocks away on Sacramento and Webster.

By the time Lorna and Matthew got there, an ER doctor had already questioned Bettina about Dante's medical history. The fall had left a bump on the little boy's head, but there really wasn't anything to worry about—

Except that his motor skills seemed slower than they should be for a child his age. From the frown on the doctor's face, she realized he suspected something was not right.

"He's fine," she insisted. "He's a Connaught, which means he has hardy ancestors. His father was a college basketball star. The child has always been perfect."

Bettina was still rattling on about him when Lorna rushed into the room. She'd never seen her sister-in-law so upset. Needless to say, she was miffed when Lorna screamed for her to get out, that she would handle the doctor's questions without any assistance, thank you very much.

Bettina was too shaken to argue. She threw off Matthew's comforting arm and ran as fast as she could out of the room and back to her car.

Of course she had noticed Dante was slower and quieter than most children his age. Still, she felt she had done the right thing by lying to the doctor about Dante's poor range of motion. Despite his mother's questionable lineage, Dante was, and always would be, a Connaught. That alone earned him her acceptance.

Besides, if the fall had caused something to be awfully wrong with Dante, she had no one to blame but herself.

This realization so upset her that her hands shook on the steering wheel as she drove back to the park. In all honesty, Jade was supposed to have been watching Dante. And why hadn't Matthew locked the stroller in place?

For that matter, Prince Vsevolod was also to blame. He'd been horrible. A nuisance! A very, very bad boy.

Oh my God, she thought. *I've left him in the park, all alone.*

The two-block distance back to the park seemed like an eternity. When she got there, she saw Lily was cradling the puppy, who was shaking like a leaf.

Lily, who had ignored Prince Vsevolod since he'd first scurried into the Cross home, was actually showing affection for the animal. Her heart soared watching Lily finally accepting him.

"Mummy, he's just a baby! Why didn't you pay attention? Why did you leave him all alone? That big mean dog was trying to eat him up!"

"I... But Dante..."

As Lily swung her head in protest, her tears flew off her cheeks. She wouldn't let Bettina cradle her. Instead, she stormed off with her puppy.

"Well, at least now they're bonding." Jade put her arm on Bettina's shoulder. "But more importantly, is Dante going to be alright? Bettina, I feel so awful! I was supposed to be watching him. How could I have been so negligent? Lorna and Matthew must hate me. And you, too! Will you ever forgive me?"

Bettina nodded. As hard as it was to admit, she felt the same way.

Poor little Dante, she thought.

"I think...I think something is seriously wrong with Dante," she whispered.

Jade didn't say a word. Instead, she opened her arms. Bettina collapsed into them.

She didn't know how long they stood there together. She should've been ashamed to have lost her composure in public, but she wasn't.

And to think, she hadn't had to tear anyone down to feel this wonderful.

"Group hug, eh? So, who's got first dibs if something pops up?"

At the sound of Art's voice, both women turned around.

Jade, embarrassed, walked away as quickly as she could.

Bettina's response was a slap.

Art rubbed his jaw as his wife walked off. "Foreplay? In public? *Awesome!*"

CHAPTER SEVENTEEN

Monday, 1 April

FOR KIMBERLEY, THE TOP MOMS POST-EASTER MEETING HAD been nothing but a series of letdowns.

No one could argue that a child in an emergency room was reason enough to leave an event one was hosting. With Bettina's blessing, Jillian, Jade, and Ally had covered for Lorna, so despite the two cartons of eggs left rotting in the sun, there had been enough to be found for the club's other forty-nine tykes, all dressed in their Easter finery.

Even Mallory declared the event a success. Kimberley presumed it had something to do with the fact that Angus Wickett found the golden egg. Rumor had it that Angus's playroom, located on the fourth floor of the Wickett mansion on the Washington Street side of Lafayette Park, was equipped with an advanced Celestron 127mm Refractor

Computerized GoTo telescope. If so, then tracking Matthew Connaught as he hid the golden egg had been child's play.

To add insult to injury, Bettina spent the rest of the meeting rhapsodizing about Jade's big get—some Nobel Prize winner who would be introducing the Fivesies to classical literature.

"And can you imagine? They're starting with *Macbeth*!" Bettina clapped her hands with glee. When she did, the puppy she now carried with her everywhere (what was its name again? Something "Prince." Or "Prince" something or other. What ev) raised its head off her lap and yawned.

Tell me about it, Kimberley thought. *Five-year-olds in kilts, butchering iambic pentameter? Make me barf now!*

No doubt Jade was a shoo-in for Top Mom. Kimberley would rather die than sit in meetings with the wife of the man she loved to hate.

Or was it that she hated to love him?

In any event, he was unquestionably the one who got away.

Well, for now.

Back home, and with the kids safely ensconced in their beds, Kimberley's pity party could begin in earnest. With a gallon-sized martini glass, forty percent of her Twinkies stash, and the latest Dildo-of-the-Month from Good Vibrations (the glass "Andromeda," with an ad that claimed it could "coax any creature from the deep"), she searched the "On-Demand" options in search of some late night porn.

Alice in Wonderlust? Ha! That sounds interesting, she thought. She clicked onto it.

When "Alice" came on the screen, Kimberley almost choked on her martini. *Jade Pierce was doing porn?*

Well, whattaya know.

Kimberley reached for the phone.

But no. Better to wait until the vote for the Top Mom, and make a grand announcement then.

After all, it was only six weeks away.

In the meantime, Kimberley would get such pleasure watching Jade be set up by Bettina as her fair-haired girl, her Second Coming.

After she burned the downloaded porn onto a DVD, she watched it. For quality control, of course. With the Andromeda in hand.

The dildo more than lived up to its reputation, even if the movie did not.

Still, it helped that the Mad Hatter's schlong was far bigger than a titmouse.

She wished her Jerry could make that same claim.

CHAPTER EIGHTEEN

Thursday, 9 May

BRADY HAD JUST PULLED INTO THE PARKING GARAGE OF Bracknell Industries when his cell phone beeped. The Caller ID came up simply as *A.*

Ally was calling him.

He screeched to a halt. The car driving up behind him did so, too, nearly ramming him. In his rearview mirror, he saw the driver mouth the word "asshole."

Brady smiled and waved an apology.

The driver, Ellis Conway, gawked at him, then slowly waved back.

Brady wasn't stupid enough to mouth what he was thinking, "asshole yourself."

He tapped his iPhone. "Hi! Good to…good to hear from you." *I sound like a lovesick schoolboy,* he chided himself.

The tone of Ally's voice was cold, distant. "I'm sorry to ask you this, but my assistant must be prepping for the board meeting because she isn't picking up my line. Would you let Laurence know I won't be coming? Zoe is sick with a fever." She laughed nervously. "Angus Wickett must have given it to her. Mallory brought him to the meet-up yesterday, and he was rubbing his hands all over her. I've got to put her in a toddler martial arts class or something, so she can protect herself from being manhandled by little hellions like Angus."

"Ally, seriously, don't worry about it. I've got you covered." He hoped he sounded casual, despite the fact his heart was pumping at the speed of a bullet train.

"Thanks, Brady. I...I truly appreciate it. On the few times I've had to miss one of these shindigs, Barry has called in as my proxy. Unfortunately, he and Christian took off for a few days, so I have no one to cover me either at home or in the office."

"Don't worry. I mean it. Go take care of Zoe."

"Thank you, Brady. Really...Thank you."

There was silence on the other end of the phone. Had she hung up? No. The seconds were still ticking away.

Every minute we spend away from each other is a minute wasted, he thought.

But before he could say that to her—or anything at all that would lead to even more pain—he hung up.

He sat in his car until he composed himself.

He hoped no one noticed his eyes were red from crying.

❧

"...SADLY, LOWER EARNINGS FOR NEXT QUARTER," LAURENCE concluded. "That's it folks, unless there are any further questions or any items that didn't make the agenda, I'll call this meeting to a close."

Ellis raised his hand. "I hate to bring up a sensitive subject, but I feel it's one that needs to be addressed immediately. Over the past quarter, one of our companies, Foot Fetish, has taken on quite a few losses. It can be attributed to over-inflated projections, coupled by poor purchasing judgment on the part of our chief buyer."

Brady couldn't believe his ears. Ellis was trying to pin his own ineffective managing on Ally. And he was succeeding. The wan smiles that most of the board members wore were flattened with the weight of their concern.

Laurence shifted uncomfortably in his seat. "Since these concerns are under Ms. Thornton's purview and she isn't here to answer your questions, why don't we shelve this for the next board meeting?"

"Frankly, that's part of the problem. I've tried on several occasions to ask her about it. She ignores all my emails. Further, she's never around to question in person. In all honesty, the number of board meetings she's missed has put her in violation of her contract."

A hum of concern rumbled through the boardroom.

"We all know Ms. Thornton well enough to consider the possibility that there is some oversight here," Brady said calmly. "Laurence, if you're motioning to wait until Ally is here to defend herself, I'll heartily second it."

"In truth, we all have lives outside this room." By the tone Ellis was using, he could have been talking to a kindergartener. "But most of us—the rest of us, in fact—don't take our roles here for granted. Foot Fetish has lost its edge. That's the reality we're facing."

A female board member, in her mid-fifties with deep auburn hair, raised her hand. "I have to say that I've personally been disappointed with their recent product lines. The company isn't a part-time hobby for a socialite. It needs a trendsetter on the helm, full-time. Someone who has her finger on the pulse of what the consumer wants today."

Brady wasn't positive, but he was sure he saw Ellis wink at the woman.

"Perhaps her new pie shop venture is taking away what little available time she has," Ellis declared.

Brady couldn't stand it anymore. "Make up your mind, Ellis. Is she a socialite hobbyist, or an over-achiever?"

"You're a good friend to Ally, Brady. But you of all people know that our loyalty is to our stockholders, first and foremost." Ellis turned to Laurence. "I'd like to motion that we buy out Ms. Thornton's contract before her half-hearted decisions cause Bracknell another quarterly loss, which will precipitate another hit on our stock price."

"I second the motion," the redhead piped up.

Only Brady and Laurence opposed the motion.

Brady was out the door the moment Laurence gaveled the meeting to a close.

He was standing at the elevator when Laurence caught up to him. "Your loyalty to Ally is admirable, Brady. I know you're here because of her, but I hope this change in direction doesn't discourage you from staying on with us."

"Ellis is lying about her. Ally cares deeply about Foot Fetish. Laurence, you need to hear this from someone who doesn't have anything to lose by saying it. She's made a lot of sacrifices, professional and personal, to ensure that the company succeeds."

Laurence shrugged. "I've always appreciated her diligence and her drive, no doubt about it. And I'm not blind. I know Ellis has an agenda. But he's right about one thing. Ally has taken herself out of the game. And if Ellis's agenda is a better one for Bracknell, it's the one we have to go with."

Brady knew he was right. If it were Brady's company, he'd feel exactly the same way.

And he would have done exactly the same thing.

To anyone but Ally.

ALLY ANSWERED BRADY'S KNOCK IN HER PAJAMAS. HER NOSE was red, and her eyes were glassy.

"You've been crying," he declared. "So, you've already heard?"

She sneezed. "I think I must have caught the same crud that has Zoe down and out. Whatever it is, it's got me too so if I fall asleep, just prop me up against the wall." Before another sneeze could escape, she blew her nose, hard. "Yuck!

Sorry...What did you say? What was I supposed to have heard?"

"You better sit down."

She shook her head and stood her ground.

"Ellis made a case for voting you off the board tonight and removing you from your job. Worse, the board bought it."

"What?" She sat down hard. "You mean I got canned?"

"You'll still get whatever golden parachute Barry wrote in for you. But yes, essentially, quote unquote, your services are no longer required."

"Well, isn't that just dandy?" She sneezed again. Then she reached for a Kleenex.

The box was empty. She held her nose with one hand and threw the box up against the wall with the other.

Quickly, he grabbed a cloth diaper from one of the two laundry baskets on the table and handed it to her. After blowing her nose on it, she threw it after the box. "Double yuck! I think that came out of the dirty laundry. But my nose is so stuffed up, I can't smell anything, so I may be wrong. Take a whiff and let me know, okay? No, never mind. I really don't want to." She threw up her hands in disgust.

"Who knows, maybe Bracknell's buyout will turn out to be a blessing in disguise. Ellis is sure to run the company into the ground, and you will have gotten your money out before he does it. And your goal was to be a stay-at-home mom, right? Besides, if the pie shop takes off the way we think it will, you'll have the entrepreneurial success you deserve, and on your own terms."

"Maybe you're right... Oh, I don't know! With this bloody fever, I can't think straight! And I'm so tired." Despite the fact that her tears were falling fast and furious, she closed her eyes. Shielding them with her hand, she added, "To top it off, I can't even call Barry to get his opinion. Those two wanted a romantic getaway, so he made it a point not to carry his cell phone with him."

Brady couldn't stand it anymore. He sat down beside her and nudged her into his arms. "You've got me. Ally, you know I'll always be here for you."

Her answer was a gentle snore. She'd fallen asleep.

He could feel her heart, pounding against his chest. Soon their hearts were beating in unison.

He wished he never had to leave her side.

That was his last thought before he too fell asleep.

JADE WAS STILL AWAKE AND SITTING IN THE ARMCHAIR FACING the front door when, right after sunrise, Brady walked into the house.

"You were with Ally, weren't you?" Her question came out in a whisper.

"It's not what you think. She had a crisis. Bracknell voted her off the board."

She shrugged. "What does that have to do with you?"

"I felt I should break the news to her in person."

"And you wanted her to know you were there for her."

He nodded.

"Well, isn't that convenient."

"Jade, you don't understand. They tore into her like a pack of hyenas. It didn't matter that she'd started the company and grew it into a huge success. They dumped her because profits slipped one lousy quarter for God's sake!" He paced the floor angrily. "It's just not fair."

He really cares for her, she thought sadly. *Everything is about Ally.*

She had to ask him. "She let you fuck her, didn't she?"

At first, he didn't answer. When finally he did, he might as well have cut her heart out with a stiletto. "You don't get it, Jade. *She's nothing like you.*"

Disgusted, he went up to his room and slammed the door behind him.

You're right, Jade thought. *She's nothing like me. If the shoe were on the other foot, I would've kept my promise to her. Instead, when she was down and out, she let you sweet-talk her.*

I know how to make her believe me, too.

Oliver's cheery morning babbling had her running up the stairs in no time. She dressed him quickly and headed back down the stairs with him so Brady wouldn't hear them take off.

It was time to pay Ally a visit.

CHAPTER NINETEEN

Friday, 10 May

"I CAME THE MOMENT I HEARD WHAT HAPPENED." JADE GAVE Ally a quick hug. "I can't believe it! Those jerks! My goodness, I hope you fight them over it."

Ally shrugged. "Thanks, Jade. It means so much to me that you're here. As for Foot Fetish, I'm so sick right now, I can't think straight. But yes, I'm pissed off."

Jade nodded sympathetically. She looked around the kitchen. Noting the tea kettle on the stove, she murmured, "Let me make some tea for us."

"That sounds nice." Ally laid her head on the tabletop. It felt cooler than her feverish forehead. She heard Jade walk over to the stove, then to the sink. As the water ran, Jade continued, "Ally, from the bottom of my heart, I want to apologize for Brady's role in your dismissal. I can't believe he'd be so cruel, so...*selfish!*"

Ally raised her head to face Jade. "What do you mean?"

Jade turned off the water. She sighed heavily before turning to face her friend. "I overheard him this morning, talking to someone at Foot Fetish. Is it Elton?...No, I remember now, Ellis. Brady said something about hating to see his chunk of stock in Bracknell losing value, and that he'd thoroughly understand if Ellis felt the need to—well, push you out. He even said he thought he could make you accept it as the best thing that could ever happen to you." She sighed. "I guess he'd rather have you focus on the pie shop. Or as he put it to Ellis, 'She thinks she can do it all, but let's face it. Being a mom is really where her head is at now.'"

So Brady sold me out, Ally thought. She dropped her head again onto the table. This time, though, she hid her face in her arms so that Jade couldn't see her cry.

Jade walked over with two cups of tea. After placing one beside, Ally, she patted her friend's bowed head and murmured, "Ally, as much as it hurts me to say so, I'm sure Brady also presumes that, with Foot Fetish out of your life, you'll have more time for him, too."

Ally lifted her head. Wiping away her tears with the back of her hand, she declared, "Ha! Well, he's wrong. I told him that door was closed, and I meant it! I'd hoped we could stay friends, but after this, I never want to see him again."

Seeing the shocked look on Jade's face, she added, "Please don't think I'm mad at you, too! Of course I'm not."

She paused contritely. "Listen, Jade. I know how hard this was for you to hear. His infatuation with me... and yes, mine with him, should never have happened. I'll regret it for as long as I live. And I'll always treasure your friendship, and your honesty."

Jade's hand shook as she picked up her teacup. Her voice shook, too, as she whispered, "Hey, that's what friends are for, right?"

CHAPTER TWENTY

Mother's Day
Sunday, 12 May
Dawn

LORNA LOVED WAKING UP TO MATTHEW'S KISSES.

To feeling him, thickened and hard, beside her.

Lately they'd all but stopped having sex. Instead, as the dawn's early light sifted through the slanted blinds over their bedroom windows, Matt lay with his back to her.

Or he wasn't in the bed at all, but slept on the couch in his home office.

It was all the proof she needed that Matt was discouraged about Dante's lack of progress.

Since Dante's fall, the little progress their son had been making in his motor skills seemed to vanish. The tests performed the next day by his autism specialist, Dr.

Remfeld, were outright discouraging. They validated Lorna's worst fears, that her son would never enjoy a truly independent life. The only issue now was the amount of functionality he could achieve.

Matt's response to the sad news was to hole up in his home office for hours on end.

In truth, his reaction to the news had dampened her passion for him, too. His helplessness was no aphrodisiac.

And yet, this morning Matt's lips found her again.

Yesterday they'd had a breakthrough with their marriage counselor.

Since he was told of Dante's condition, their sessions usually started with stormy silences, but invariably ended in shouting matches. Yesterday, Lorna felt it was her duty to point out all the ways in which he ignored both her and Dante, to remind him he was in denial. He countered by accusing her of always expecting too much from everyone, most certainly him.

"I guess you'll be pushing Dante all the harder to prove he isn't autistic after all!" Matt had growled. "Admit it, Lorna. You're the one in denial."

Upon hearing this, she burst into tears.

When her sobs finally subsided, she realized he was cradling her in his arms.

He whispered over and over, "Don't cry, Lorna, please don't cry. We'll both be strong for Dante. Together. Always together."

For the first time since Dante's fall, they'd fallen asleep in each other's arms.

Now, hearing her sigh and seeing her smile, his mouth moved lower, nuzzling her throat, roaming below her shoulders before zigzagging toward the nearest breast, her left one. As his tongue slowly circled her nipple, a surge of desire swept over her. fully aroused, she took his hand and led it inside of her. At the same time, she placed her hand around his dick. It was already stiff. Her touch brought a moan to his lips, and deeper thrusts from his forefinger and thumb.

Feeling her moistness, her readiness to accept him, he mounted her, murmuring something. His voice was so low that she could not make out his words, but his tone was one of love and longing. Her moans, coming in tandem with his, were even louder. But her whispers, though dampened with her tears of joy, were naughty. Filthy, really. She begged for the kind of pain that comes with unrequited lust; for the need to be forgiven.

Each thrust was that, and more.

Finally, he collapsed on her, spent.

No. He was broken. "My son will never know a woman in this way. He will never be a normal man, living a normal life," he whispered. There was just enough light to see the dampness on his cheeks.

She had to forgive him because as she climaxed, she'd had exactly the same thought.

She was crying about it, too.

11: 10 a.m.

"I DON'T KNOW WHY YOU FEEL THE NEED TO DRESS THESE TWO alike!" Jillian's mother, Beverly, sniffed. "I can never tell them apart."

Jillian frowned. It was a silly thing to do, but Jillian loved dressing Addison and Amelia exactly alike, especially for something as special as Mother's Day.

"Of course they're different," she countered. "Amelia is taller, and her hair is a shade darker. And Addison's dimple is on the right side."

She reached for Addison's hand, which now held a butter knife. Gently, she extracted it from the little girl's chubby fingers. "You know, Mother, if you spent more time with them, you'd see these things too."

"Ha! That's just your way of trying to get me to babysit for free." Beverly's guffaw echoed through Gamine's, the cozy little French bistro on Union Street that Jillian had chosen to take Beverly for Mother's Day.

They had strolled down to the restaurant from Jillian's house, stopping at the Life of Pie along the way. Jillian was proud of the fact that the place was bustling. The line was out the door with customers waiting to pick up their pies.

Appropriately enough, a favorite on the menu was the pie she'd created in honor of her mother. Called Very Berry Beverly, its filling boasted four juicy fruits: blueberry, blackberry, raspberry, and cranberry. For an added bit of tartness, it also had lemon zest.

Earlier in the day, she'd dropped one off at Gamine's, so that it could be served to her mother after their meal, as a special surprise.

Jillian turned to Beverly. "Isn't this great?"

Her mother shrugged. "I think it's a lot of work for someone with two babies. You look even more exhausted than the last time I saw you. Now I know why."

Jillian bit her tongue to keep from lashing out at her mother. *Yes, I'm bone tired,* she wanted to say. *But unlike you, who has never worked a day in her life and collects alimony, I'm making my own way.* But, of course, she said none of that.

Instead, she forced a smile on her face and said, "Yes, my life is full these days. And I'm happy, too. Which is what you want for me, isn't it, Mother?"

Her mother's nod was more like a reluctant shrug.

Jillian ignored it. "Shall we continue on to lunch?"

As always, Gamine's mussels had been divine. The girls had shared a plate of scrambled eggs.

Beverly deemed the restaurant's signature omelet "just so so," but Jillian couldn't help but notice that her mother had cleaned her plate, which had included merguez sausage, gruyere cheese, caramelized onions, and harissa.

Jillian smiled. "Now, how about a little dessert with our coffee? There's something special here I'd like you to try."

Her mother nodded warily. "Nothing too rich. I'm watching my weight. You know better than anyone that men like their women slim and fun."

"What's that supposed to mean?"

"Don't play coy. I know why you jog as hard as you do. And from the look of you, you're certainly not eating any of your own pies." She leaned in conspiratorially. "Too bad. But

I guessed you learned the hard way that a bird in the hand is worth two in the bush."

"Mother, I have absolutely no idea what you're talking about." With just a second to spare, Jillian grabbed a dessert fork from Amelia before she had a chance to stab her sister with it. "Try English. It's my native language."

"I was just curious if you'd ever…well, you know, gotten tired of Scott, the way he tired of you."

"Scott cheated on me, Mother. Plain and simple. Let's call it what it is."

"Yes, dear, but that's usually a sign of boredom in the bedroom." Her mother's smirk was irritating. "During ten years of marriage, weren't you ever bored?"

Jillian shifted her gaze to the other restaurant patrons around them. Most were mothers with sons and daughters and husbands.

If things had been different, Scott would be here right now. He barely put up with Beverly, but he'd see her if Jillian insisted.

"His brother—what was his name again? Oh yes, Jeff. He was a cutie. Didn't he stay with the two of you one summer?"

Jillian turned back to Beverly. "What are you implying?"

Beverly pursed her lips. "Nothing. Quit acting so guilty."

"I'm not acting guilty!" Hearing the tone of their mother's voice, the twins froze from the game they'd created—tossing sugar packs at each other—and turned to stare at Jillian. Before their wariness turned to frightened tears, she lifted her mouth into a smile. "Mother, why did you bring up Jeff?"

"I...oh, just forget about it!" She waved to the waiter. "Tell him to skip the coffee. I'd prefer a martini."

Jillian slapped her mother's hand down. Seeing this, the twins squealed with laughter. They slapped hands, too. Patty cake was a game they loved.

"No! No liquor," Jillian hissed at Beverly. "Not until you tell me what little game you're playing." Jillian knew gin, with a whisper of vermouth, was akin to mother's milk to Beverly. Having been cut off from it all afternoon, there was nothing for Beverly to do but come clean.

Beverly shrugged. "Quit being so dramatic! I told the private eye he was barking up the wrong tree."

"What private eye? What are you talking about?"

"The one Scott sent over. Somehow I guess he's under the impression that he can buy my loyalty."

"You mean he offered you a bribe?"

"Not a bribe exactly... Okay well, yes, there was to be some quid pro quo. But only if I could validate his theory that you and Jeff...well, I don't want to say it in front of the children."

"I'm not afraid to shout it from the rooftops!" Jillian stood up, furious. "Here's what you can tell Scott. I did not fuck his brother! And my daughters are his, too!"

To make her point, she threw her hand back. Unknowingly, she slapped the waiter who was bringing the Very Berry Beverly pie for Jillian to present to her mother.

The man dropped the pie in Beverly's lap. It was hot enough that Beverly yelped.

Before she could stand up, Jillian grabbed the girls and stormed out of the restaurant.

The whole way home, they cried for pie.

She knew she had none in the house, but she didn't want to stop back at the shop for one. She just wanted to get home, put the girls down for their naps, and bury her head under her pillows.

Had things been different, had Scott not deserted her for Victoria, he'd have at least bought her flowers.

No, at the most he would've skipped his usual Sunday game of golf.

And he would have groused about it the whole day.

Either way, she would have had a lousy Mother's Day.

She was shocked to see him waiting for her, on the stoop of her house—not Scott, but Caleb.

And not with flowers, but with a pie.

From the box, she knew it was from her shop. He held it out to her. "It's the girls' favorite, 'ah-poo.' I had to fight off three desperate husbands for it, but you're worth it."—he shrugged and smiled—"I missed you, Jillian. And... I love you. But we both know I'm not him. And I'll never be him."

Jillian threw herself into his arms. Between kisses, she whispered, "Is that a promise? Please say yes!"

The only ones who seemed to care when the pie box dropped to the ground were the twins, who cried until Jillian put it between them and let them go at it.

She was too busy to care.

1:05 p.m.

"Brussels sprouts! My favorite!" Hera Harmony smiled across the table at her hostess, Eleanor Morrow Connaught. "Our daughters have honored us with quite a groaning board of delicacies, have they not?"

She nodded toward the rest of the bowls and platters on the sideboard. There was grilled eggplant, wild rice, barbecued salmon, and a generous spinach salad that seemed to have barely been touched, despite the amount of food dished onto the plates of all at the table—the Connaughts, the Crosses, all the children and their mothers.

She was right. The sisters-in-law had made an obvious attempt at providing a meal that would be appreciated by a mother who was rabidly vegan, and another who, at least publicly, pretended to follow her cardiologist's heart-healthy diet to a tee.

Her hostess raised her wine glass. "The sweetest part of the meal is sharing it with you, Hera. And thank you for agreeing to share your daughter with us today."

Hera's smile withered into a smirk. "But you see her many times during the week, don't you? That said, the toast should be the other way around. Thank you for sharing her with me."

Lorna glanced sharply at her mother. *Please keep your promise and don't let anything get under your skin,* she begged silently. *Just another hour or two, and it will be over. This wretched day will finally come to an end.*

Out of the corner of her eye, Lorna watched as Art nudged Bettina. This prompted a ghost of a smile from his wife.

I guess Bettina is about to get her wish. What a perfect Mother's Day for her, if for none of the rest of us.

Eleanor leaned back in her chair. Lorna had learned to read her body language early in their relationship. In that one offhanded barb, Hera obliterated two hours of gentle chitchat, glowing compliments, and gracious condescension. "If Lorna spends an inordinate amount of time with us Connaughts, one can only assume she enjoys our company."

Hera shrugged. "My daughter has had a lifelong affinity of seeking out conflict. From what I can see, there's plenty of it here."

"I beg your pardon?" Eleanor's eyebrows rose almost to her ice white widow's peak. "I imagine Lorna finds our family a haven, compared to her tempestuous storm of a childhood! Your structureless hippy lifestyle isn't the most calming for young minds and hearts."

"Mummy, what's a hippy?" Lily yanked Bettina's sleeve for attention.

"What? Oh…Do you remember those scary old people in rags who we see when we venture into the park beyond the DeYoung Museum?"

The little girl nodded slowly as the vision came to her. "You mean, the ones who are always begging for loose change?"

"Yes, dear." Bettina held up a finger to shush her daughter.

Lily shook her head adamantly. "But Daddy told me those people were bums."

"Same thing," Art muttered under his breath.

"Is that what you tell the keepers of our future, that 'hippies' are bums? That the brave souls who brought about Civil Rights and women's liberation and the end to a ridiculous war are nothing but loony panhandlers?" Hera asked. "What elitists!"

"In all fairness, you've just brought the term 'loony panhandlers' into the conversation," Art pointed out. "However, if the Birkenstock fits, feel free to steal it."

Hera glared at him. "Your aura is pitch black!"

He nodded to the rest of the group. "And she's a racist to boot! If I happened to be African-American, I might actually be offended. I rest my case."

"I was referring to the color of your soul! Talk about aura blockage! No wonder Dante is autistic!"

Eleanor eyes flashed angrily. "What did you say about my grandson?"

"You say you love him, and you're around him almost every day! And yet, you're so blind to his condition! How can that be?"

Seeking the answer to this conundrum, Hera turned to Lorna.

Eleanor's eyes followed hers to Lorna's as well.

Lorna looked from one to the other. After what seemed like an eternity, she stood up and lifted Dante out of his high chair. Holding him to her chest, she turned to Eleanor. "It's true. I suspected something was wrong about eight months ago. The tests are ongoing. Thus far, the results haven't been good. Dante has been going to a specialist. The best in the state when it comes to diagnosing autism in babies. You know him. Dr. Remfeld."

"Remfeld?" Eleanor's voice trembled. "I've donated generously to his department. The least he could have done was—"

"Eleanor, please don't hold anything against Dr. Remfeld," Lorna pleaded. "He's been very good to Dante. And in his defense, he's been encouraging me to break the news to the family from the very beginning."

"'Family.' I guess in your mind that doesn't mean us Connaughts, just *her*!" Eleanor stood up. "After all we've done for you, Lorna, you take it upon yourself to hide this from us? From me?"

"Eleanor, you don't understand."

"Don't… patronize me. At least grant me that." Eleanor stood up. "Please feel free to show yourselves out."

She walked out of the room. Her heavy footsteps could be heard climbing the grand staircase.

Lily ran after her.

Slowly, Lorna walked out of the house with Dante.

Matthew ran out after them.

Hera looked at Bettina. "Happy Mother's Day. I think you got exactly what you wanted."

2:30 p.m.

"HERE'S TO THE BEST MOTHER IN THE WORLD!" CHRISTIAN TOOK the last of the champagne and poured it into Ally's empty glass.

"Really I shouldn't! I've already had too much." She giggled, then stuck a pinky finger into the sticky liquid and swirled it around. Watching her, Zoe did the same, only in Barry's champagne glass.

Barry shrugged, then lifted her fingers to his mouth and pretended to eat them. The little girl squealed with delight.

Barry turned to Ally. "It's your day! You can do anything you damn well please. Besides, you're not driving. You're in the privacy of your own home."

"Really, it's your home. I live next door." Ally's giggle sounded silly and far away. She caught herself in the mirror over the breakfront and smiled as wide as she could. "What would you call this, 'drunk smiling?'"

Christian snickered. "As long as it isn't drunk dialing." He moved toward the window and opened a blind. A beam of sunshine splashed over the teardrop crystals of the dining room chandelier, making a rainbow on the ceiling.

Zoe cooed as she reached up over her head.

Ally, too, was entranced.

Ally wagged a finger at him. "Oh, no. I've never done that in my life. Don't see the point. When I humiliate myself, I'm totally sober. It's smarter to remember every gory detail." She sat up straight and proud. "Gives you a reason to lick your wounds and regroup. It's made me the woman I am today."

Christian moved away from the window. "Speaking of humiliation, Brady is out front, again, ringing your doorbell. This time with two dozen roses."

"Ignore him, Christian," Barry warned.

Christian stamped his foot in frustration. "But he's so pathetic, the way he comes loping around, begging to see our girl." He turned to Barry, all pouty eyes. "Have a heart already."

"They're two of a kind," Ally growled. "Brady doesn't have a heart, either." She looked down at her chest. "And neither do I." To make sure she was right, she peeked under her blouse. "I can't hear it. So I guess it's broken."

Barry and Christian's doorbell was different than Ally's. It rivaled Big Ben's chimes in tone, if not clarity.

"Omigod, too loud! It's giving me a headache!" Ally put her hands over her ears. "Make him stop, please!"

Barry rapped on the window and yelled, "Go away! She doesn't want to see you!"

But the doorbell kept chiming. Only Zoe found it funny.

"I can't stand it any longer," Christian shouted. He opened the door.

Brady seemed surprised.

Even more so when Christian took the roses out of his hand, and shut the door again, locking it firmly.

He looked down at the bouquet. "I was wrong. Make that *three* dozen roses."

He tossed the bouquet at Ally, who caught it with both

hands. "Ow! Bloody thorns!" She tossed them onto the table and sucked her wound.

The doorbell's chimes now sounded like a Westminster royal wedding had just ended.

"My turn," Ally declared. She rose and stumbled to the front door. Before Barry could stop her, she opened it.

The next moment, she was gone.

Silence.

Barry and Christian looked at each other and shrugged. "Well, at least we can hear ourselves think again."

They clinked glasses, then filled them again.

*

Now that Ally was actually face-to-face with him, Brady didn't know what to say. Finally, he stuttered, "Why won't you take my calls?"

Ally wrapped her arms around her waist. Glaring at him, she muttered, "Why can't you take a hint?"

He couldn't believe his ears. "After what I did for you, the least you owe me is an explanation."

"Owe you?" She stood up straight. "Tell you what—I'll infiltrate your boardroom, diss you to its members, and sell you down the river. Then we'll call it even!"

"What the hell are you talking about?"

"You don't think I know what you did at Bracknell, how you stood by Ellis, and against me?"

She came at him, both fists flailing.

He fought the instinct to raise his hands to cover his chest from her blows. When finally she stopped, exhausted, he held her close and whispered in her ear, "Ally, that's not true. In fact, I quit the board, too. The very next day."

She raised her head and sought out his eyes. "You did?...But Jade said…"

He frowned. "What did she say?"

"That you were in cahoots with Ellis. That you encouraged him to kick me off." She gulped hard, but she choked nonetheless when she added, "I thought you'd quit believing in me."

He shook his head. "Never." He put her down gently on the porch bench. "And I'll never stop believing in us, either. But you have to believe in us, too."

Before she could answer him, before she could ask him to forgive her and tell him she loved him, he was gone.

By the time she got back into the house, that prism rainbow had disappeared, too.

3:14 p.m.

"PLEASE DON'T SLAM THE DOOR IN MY FACE." *OF COURSE IF Eleanor does, I can't blame her,* Lorna thought.

Her mother-in-law shrugged. "The drama queens live in the Castro. This is Pacific Heights, dear. We try our best to be civil."

She stood aside so that Lorna could enter.

For the past two hours, Lorna had been composing her

thoughts. But now that she was standing in front of Eleanor, the lump in her throat kept the words from coming out.

Until Eleanor asked, "Do you hate me that much?"

"No! Oh no, please!"

Then the words and emotions came tumbling out and over each other. She described how, since their very first meeting, she'd felt intimidated by Eleanor. How she felt she'd never measure up or be accepted, no matter how much she loved Matthew.

No matter how much he loved her back.

She was quite aware that Eleanor's acceptance came with a heavy price, her sister-in-law's resentment.

And she admitted her biggest fear was that Eleanor would blame her for Dante's condition.

Or worse yet, blame Dante for being a blemish on the Connaught line.

When she was done, Eleanor didn't speak at first.

Finally, she reached for Lorna's hand and squeezed it. "I'll be the first to admit that we Connaughts are an intimidating clan." She held out her arms for Dante.

Lorna gave him up.

Then she gave Eleanor a hug.

Suddenly the lump was back in Lorna's throat. "Now that Bettina knows...."

"Now that Bettina knows, she'll do what she can to make her nephew always feel loved and accepted," Eleanor declared. "I'll see to that."

3:33 p.m.

"Pack up. You're out of here."

"What?" Jade didn't look away from the television. She was too enthralled with the Borgia brothers, who were snarling at each other while a naked wench lay on a bed between them.

At C.R.'s suggestion, she was doing her best to delve into the classics, but she found Shakespeare a bore. Masterpiece Theatre came in a close second. At least HBO and Showtime's take on history was leavened with some spicy sex scenes. She loved well-defined men in tights. She loved them even more out of them.

When Jade didn't respond, Brady dragged her off the couch, onto the floor. Watching from his playpen, Oliver put all his fingers in his mouth and started to whine.

Jade scrambled out of reach. "What the hell do you think you're doing?"

"I'm kicking you out. I said grab your stuff, and I meant it. I've called a taxi. It'll take you to the airport. You're out of here, now."

"But...why—?"

"You know why. Because you lied to Ally! You told her I was in cahoots with that creep Ellis!"

"Yes, okay, I admit it. I told her all that, and more. And I'm not a bit sorry. Quite frankly, you should be thanking me. She'll never love you like I do. You're mooning after someone who'll never appreciate you." Jade stood up, her head held high. "Do you know what? She never even questioned it! Ask yourself, Brady. Why did she find it so easy to believe such awful things about you? Don't you get it? She knows that, deep down inside, you are totally despicable."

He raised his hand to slap her.

She didn't flinch. She didn't move a muscle. In fact, she hoped he would hit her. Because then he'd hate himself for doing so. And he'd take her in his arms and say he was sorry.

Once she was in his arms, she knew what to do so that he'd never let go of her, ever again.

Instead, he lowered his arm. "Don't you get it, Jade? I'll never love *you* like you love me. I'll never appreciate *you*. And right now, I only despise you."

He picked up Oliver and walked up the stairs.

She heard the lock on his bedroom door turn and click.

Right now, he said. But 'right now' wasn't forever.

No, she wasn't going to move out. Her home was here. She'd done exactly what Brady had asked of her, so he'd have to put up with her.

She'd made herself a part of the club. The last thing she was going to do was give that up.

She grabbed her purse and her keys and walked to the door.

It was time to buy a little insurance.

4: 20 p.m.

"I HAVE A CONFESSION TO MAKE," JADE BEGAN. HER VOICE WAS shaking.

Bettina yawned. "Make it snappy. It's Mother's Day, remember? My family needs me."

In truth, she had Art trussed up against the upholstered tuffet in their master suite.

Not everyone had walked away feeling that the gathering at Eleanor's had been a fiasco. She for one was elated with how things went.

Granted, it saddened her to learn of Dante's autism. She could see how much it upset her beloved brother.

Even Lily was aware that Dante needed extra loving. She had insisted on going home with Uncle Matthew "until Dante gets well" is how she put it.

Bettina didn't have the heart to tell her that he would never get better.

Hera had been right. The best gift she'd received all day was getting under that old hippy's skin. Metaphorically, that is. Physically was too grotesque to even consider, as it was obvious the woman hadn't used sun block a single day of her life.

Okay, make that the second best thing to happen today. Watching her mother blow up at Lorna certainly took the prize.

On the way home, Bettina squealed with delight. "I did it! Finally! I can ax Lorna from the club and Mother won't give a hoot!"

"What excuse will you use?"

"Simple. She hid Dante's condition. That's a club no-no.

Granted, there may be some outcry about political incorrectness. But I've got a good answer for that." She lowered her lashes, as if practicing her spiel. "Even the best-bred children can be cruel sometimes. Almost always, in fact. I'm sure the Top Moms will agree with me that it's for his own good that he join a group with children who will be more accepting of him."

"Brilliant!" Art declared.

Bettina lowered her voice to a sultry growl. "Do you really think so?"

"No. It sucks." His lips raised into a naughty smirk.

She slapped him in the face. "You'll pay for saying that."

He lowered his head. "Yes, my mistress."

She was in the middle of making good on this promise when Jade showed up.

"I have very bad news related to the club," Jade murmured. "But please, Bettina, no one must know this information came from me."

Bettina sighed. "My lips are sealed."

"Brady was invited onto a corporation board—Bracknell Industries. To my surprise – to my *dismay* – Ally Thornton also sits on the board."

Bettina shrugged. "We all belong to some status board or another. For the most part they are honorary positions."

"No, you don't get it." Jade leaned in closer. "She's on the board because she's an employee and an officer of one of their companies. She's the founder of Foot Fetish. She still goes in two days a week on the days we don't have meetups, of course. Or at least, she was until recently."

"So, you're telling me she held this position when she applied to the club?" Bettina frowned. "If so, then you're right. Our feelings about working moms may be unspoken, but they apply to everyone equally. To have lied about it during the application process was egregious."

"Bettina, it gets worse. Turns out Ally's not even married! Her so-called husband is really her attorney and her sperm donor. Her *gay* sperm donor."

Oh. My. God.

"Are you positive?"

"Yes. I mean, Barry's a nice enough guy. But he's just a beard so that she could get into the club. The facts are the facts. There is no record of their marriage. You can check it out yourself."

Aw hell. Getting rid of one member was a scandal. Getting rid of two might start a wild exodus. Everyone would be sweating whether their dirty laundry would be aired next. Bettina's own panties were down around Art's ankles, along with his pants.

She'd waited too long to get rid of Lorna. Ally's indiscretion would have to be dealt with at a later date.

Not that Jade needed to know that. "Okay, Jade dear, you've done your duty. Earned major brownie points, yada yada."

"So, Ally is out?" Jade was actually trembling at the thought.

"Yes...but maybe not immediately. All in good time, dearie. All in good time."

She shut the door on Jade's shocked face.

Bettina was halfway up the stairs when her phone rang. Caller ID showed it was Eleanor. She groaned. Why now, of all times?

Of course, she had to pick it up. "Darling, we need to talk." Eleanor's voice was all sweetness and light.

"Mother?" Bettina tried to match her mother's happy tone. "Yes, but...well, I was in the middle of washing my hair."

"This won't take long," Eleanor promised.

She was right. In less than sixty seconds, Eleanor explained in no uncertain terms, why any thoughts Bettina may have regarding Dante's elimination from PHM&T might affect Eleanor's support of Lily's ballet lessons ("both stateside and abroad," she emphasized) as well as the little girl's trust fund.

"She can join you in living off whatever pittance Art provides," Eleanor warned.

By the time the call ended, Bettina was so angry she couldn't see straight. When she got through with Art, he wouldn't be able to able to walk upright.

There would certainly be some drama at the Top Moms meeting tomorrow.

Unfortunately, that drama would have nothing to do with Lorna Connaught.

CHAPTER TWENTY-ONE

Monday, 13 May
10:24 a.m.

"So, let me get this straight. She's married to a gay man?" Sally Dunder shook her head, confused. "I know straight men are in short supply in this town, but still…"

Joanna groaned, then covered her mouth. "Oh my God! One of the librarians may overhear us!" She was right. Except for the Top Moms, the Golden Gate Valley Branch was as quiet as a tomb. "A more important question," she whispered, "is why any gay man in San Francisco would want to marry a straight woman. I mean come on already. If the closet door is wide open in any town, it's this one."

"You two are idiots," Mallory growled. "Their charade was to ensure she got into the club. Well, I for one am outraged!"

"Me too," murmured Kimberley. *Yes! Yes! Brady's crush was getting kicked out of the club! Yes!*

Once the rest of the Top Moms heard Jade's little secret, Kimberley's day would be complete.

To top it off, Brady's love life would be completely over.

And yet, if he needed her to lick his wounds—or anything else—Kimberley would be there at his side in a second.

"Then the vote is unanimous. Ally Thornton applied for membership under false pretenses and was admitted under the same. Unacceptable! All in favor?"

The yeas were given all around, three with gusto and the other four in stunned dismay.

"Now, on to other business. The AP Classes seem to be top notch—"

"Bettina, sorry to interrupt." Kimberley sighed. "Unfortunately, I have another bit of bad news. It turns out we have yet another liar in our midst." From her purse she pulled out the bootlegged DVD of *Alice in Wonderlust*. "To my disgust, this *porn* video stars one of our own." She waited until the gasps subsided before adding, "Jade Pierce."

This time there was only one gasp, Bettina's.

Fabulous, Kimberley thought. *But of course, porn is the biggest disgrace of all.*

Bettina's eyes grew wide. Kimberley felt as if she were watching an animal trying to figure out a way to escape a trap.

Wow, I guess she's upset that this may reflect on the club as a

*whole. To put her at ease, I'll lead the Top Moms in a vow of silence
about the matter. It'll go away in no time. And so will Jade.*

She was just about to make this suggestion when Bettina
smacked the gavel. "Whereas I'm sure we all agree with
Kimberley that Jade's indiscretion is disgusting, perverted,
and unfortunate, I feel we must reflect on her actions
in toto."

Sally frowned. "You mean, like the dog in *The Wizard
of Oz*?"

Kimberley sighed loudly, then put the video into one of
the library's desktop computers, but muted the sound the
moment the grunts and groans of the actors began. Bettina
stared at the lewd acts on display so intently that Kimberley
was wondering if she was taking mental notes.

Finally, Bettina stopped the video to the disappointment
of the others. "First off, it was so grainy, how do we really
know this is Jade?"

"Because it says so on the cover," Kimberley argued.
"Right there, see? 'Starring Jade Pennypacker.' She was
stupid enough to use her first name."

"True." Bettina nodded thoughtfully. "But we all make
mistakes. In this case, by the copyright date we know it was
made before she joined us. And nowhere in the bylaws does
it say 'Thou shalt not have starred in a porno movie.'"

"I object!" Mallory hissed. "Are you telling me we're
going to let her slide on this...this perversity?"

Bettina nodded. "In this very special case, I'm willing to,
yes. In fact, I like the cut of her jib. Her meteoric rise in the
club is the culmination of so many wonderful accomplish-

ments! Answer me this. Who else scored a Nobel Prize winner for a PHM&T advanced placement class?"

Noting the looks of horror on everyone's faces, she sighed. "Okay bottom line—we can't afford any scandals at any time, let alone two scandals in one week."

Kimberley knew Bettina was right, but that didn't make her any happier.

Well there's one consolation prize, Kimberley thought. *With Jade around, Brady can't be far behind.*

Thank goodness that bitch Ally is at least out of the way.

11:30 a.m.

THE AXING WAS ANYTHING BUT SUBTLE. ACCOMPANIED BY THE other Top Moms, Bettina sauntered up to the Alta Plaza Park playground and made the announcement in front of the entire playgroup.

Ally was stoic about it. Head held high, she put Zoe in her stroller and rolled her out of the playground.

The other Onesies stood there, stunned.

What Bettina wasn't counting on was Jillian pulling her girls out of the sandbox, strapping them into their stroller, and walking away.

The nerve of her, Bettina fumed.

But what really made Bettina's blood boil was Lorna's reaction. She grabbed Dante and followed Jillian down the hill.

Considering your own dirty little secret, I'd think you'd be grateful for my discretion, Bettina thought.

She turned to Jade. Had the two of them been alone, Bettina would have slapped her silly. *That little whore almost caused a mutiny,* she fumed. *Not to mention the Top Moms think I'm a fool for protecting her! She owes me, big time. And I know just how I'll make her pay.*

Smiling supremely, she patted Jade on the back. "Now you're *really* one of us, my dear. Welcome to the club!"

Jade tried to smile, but she couldn't. She'd never felt lonelier in her life.

—To Be Continued—

NEXT UP!

TOTLANDIA: Book 4 (The Onesies/Summer)

Summer sizzles in Totlandia, emotions boil over. When Jillian's vindictive joke backfires, she learns the true meaning of forgiveness. Jade's betrayal puts her in a dangerous downward spiral with no bottom in sight—until she finds friendship and redemption where she least expects it. Lorna faces the biggest trial in her marriage, and makes an important decision that may end it for good. While Ally may regret the choices made she to get accepted in the club, her exile puts new opportunities in her path, thanks to Brady and his ceaseless desire to win her over—with Barry's help, who is playing his own little game with the Top Moms Committee. But it's Bettina who suffers the ultimate punishment—one that changes her life, and the livelihood of the club, forever.

The Housewife Assassin's Deadly Dossier (Book 15: The Series Prequel)

The Housewife Assassin's Greatest Hits (Book 16)

More Josie Brown Novels

The Candidate

Secret Lives of Husbands and Wives

The Baby Planner

HOW TO REACH JOSIE

To write Josie, go to:
mailfromjosie@gmail.com

To find out more about Josie, or to get on her eLetter list for
book launch announcements, go to her website:
www.JosieBrown.com

You can also find her at:

www.AuthorProvocateur.com

twitter.com/JosieBrownCA

facebook.com/josiebrownauthor

pinterest.com/josiebrownca

instagram.com/josiebrownnovels

Made in the USA
Middletown, DE
14 April 2018